Addicted To
Vengeance

Addicted To Vengeance
First Edition July 2023
Edited By: Christine Morgan
Cover Illustration By: Christy Aldridge
(Grim Poppy Design)

Addicted To Vengeance

By Stephen Cooper

Splatploitation Press

Splatploitation Press

www.splatploitation.com
https://www.youtube.com/@Splatploitation
https://splatploitation.substack.com

Vengeance

It hadn't been easy hacking off the arm with an eroded crowbar, but Barrett was a persistent motherfucker.

After everything the three assholes had done to him, they warranted maximum pain. Extreme punishment! Barrett deserved his vengeance, and by God was he going to have it. The three scumbags had taken away nearly two years of Barrett's life; that's how long he estimated it took him to be fully fit and healthy again. To be able to fucking walk again. Two years! Sure, they'd served six for their crimes, but in Barrett's estimation it wasn't nearly enough, so he'd taken it upon himself to be judge, jury, and executioner.

Copeland was the dead slime-ball missing an arm. The weasel of the three. The one who would have died a long time ago if he wasn't friends with the other two. It would have either been an overdose of whatever shit he seemed to be permanently on - despite having no choice but to get clean in prison - or, some other asshole would have brutally ended the loudmouth dickhead.

His dad should have pulled out and shot over his mum's tits. As none of those things happened, his life was sadistically extinguished by Barrett instead.

Barrett hadn't planned on killing Copeland first; he was just the unfortunate piece of shit who left the other two's side, so jumped the queue. He'd needed a piss, and now had no arm to aim his pathetic shrivelled pecker with; no heartbeat either.

Apparently, clawing an arm off with a rusty crowbar could kill a man. *The more you know.* The repeated blows to his emaciated head probably hadn't helped, nor using the crowbar to tear his meth-rotten teeth from his diseased mouth. It could have been the stomps to the heart as well, or the fact Barrett had unsuccessfully tried to get to the ticker with the crowbar.

He'd made a right fucking mess of the human excrement. But fuck him. He was a rapist scumbag who thought it was funny to assault woman. A cunty little fuck-face who laughed and whooped as he'd beat on Barrett beside his mates, just because Barrett tried to help the poor girl.

And he had helped her. If it wasn't for Barrett, she'd have got three hungry dicks in her instead of only ripped clothes and a black eye. He'd arrived just in time to save her, but had paid the price for the heroics.

They'd stomped the holy-hell out of him. Broke his cheekbone. Knocked several of his teeth out. Dislodged his left eye, which thankfully had been put back where it belonged and was mostly functioning fine now. They'd broken one of his arms, dislocated a shoulder, and viciously shattered both his kneecaps to the point that him not being able to walk again seemed like a real possibility.

They'd fucked up a bunch of other stuff too, but the list was too long for Barrett to remember, and the concussion didn't help. The doctors had been pessimistic about his chance of a full recovery, but Barrett was a tough son-of-a-bitch.

He may not have looked it at first glance. Barrett often came across as average in a lot of ways. Ordinary, barring the remaining scarring from the beatings, and the crooked nose which couldn't be fully set. But beneath his distinctly average face was a ripped guy with a ridiculously high pain tolerance. Someone who could take a fucking beating and not stay down, which is probably why they beat on him for such a prolonged period.

He hadn't dished anything out beside pushing them off the helpless woman, but he could take it. And take it. And take it. A lesser man may have died at their ruthless hands. They would have got a lot more time in the slammer if that was the case, but

Barrett's toughness meant they were out in six, and then he could finally exact his vengeance.

Barrett left the bathroom of the rundown squalor and turned a few corners to hear the other two bastards laughing, in-between the claps of thunder exploding outside the building.

The same irritating, throaty laughs they'd displayed at full volume while battering him. While breaking his bones, and promising the defenceless woman they'd get back to her; *thankfully they never did.* Barrett could have picked the heinous laughs from a line-up. They haunted his dreams, although haunted wasn't the right word. It wasn't like he'd suffered some kind of post traumatic stress disorder. More like, motivated his dreams. Encouraged his revenge. And now the annoying fucking laughs marked his targets, giving him their exact position so he could strike.

But Barrett didn't need to sneak up on the lowlife scum, and had no intention of doing so, as he walked into the filthy den holding the bloody crowbar in hand. Some of Copeland's arm meat and viscera still clung to the claw of the now crimson-painted bar. He wanted them to know the crowbar had seen action. He wanted them to ask what he fuck. They didn't disappoint.

"What the fuck?" the bigger of the two remaining men, *Jay,* snapped, as he saw the gory weapon.

Barrett hadn't known the fuckers' names until pretty much the day he testified against them. He hadn't wanted to testify, despite the beatdown, but there had been multiple witnesses, and the dicks had been caught the same night. Whatever his reasons for not wanting to testify were ignored. These fuckers were going down, and Barrett had been in no state to immediately deliver his vengeance anyway.

Jay was a big man who'd bulked up even more in prison. He could handle himself in a fight too, but had been downing beers all night. They'd all lost everything when they ended up in the joint, but that was no reason not to celebrate their freedom, which is exactly what they'd been doing. Pounding back the beers and talking about all the bitches they were going to fuck. Although, it would have to be consensual for the time-being, as they couldn't risk going straight back to the big house.

The beer had slurred Jay's words, but Barrett didn't know yet whether it would affect his ability to throw a punch. He wasn't going to wait to find out.

The sound of thick raindrops from the storm outside crashing against the boarded windows of the abandoned building was joined by the loud vicious thud of Barrett's crowbar connecting with Jay's face.

The big man barely had time to react as he loosely got a hand up to soften the blow. All he succeeded in doing was getting his wrist broken, as well as his orbital socket cracked. The behemoth dropped to one knee, trying to hold both his face and broken wrist with the remaining hand; he still wasn't sure what the fuck was happening. A smash to the top of his skull with the crowbar temporarily ended such thoughts as he was knocked the hell out.

Richard, the last of the three men, was slow to react as Barrett took down his buddy. He'd been the one with his long noodle-thin cock already out on the day Barrett saved the woman, and therefore had been the most disappointed with Barrett's bravery. *Cost him pussy.*

He'd taken a piss on Barrett as compensation, while Copeland and Jay laid into him. There'd even been an amusing moment where Jay got annoyed as Richard accidentally pissed on his boot while he was stomping on Barrett. Barrett hadn't been in on the joke; he was too busy getting his ass kicked.

"Fuck you do that for!?" Richard roared, clearly not having the slightest idea who Barrett was.

4

Barrett suspected they wouldn't remember him. They didn't seem the type who would. More wrapped up in their own little world, playing the victim. *Why should they get time in prison when they didn't even get their dicks wet?*

How the hell they only got six years was anyone's guess, but it was to Barrett's advantage the justice system was fucked. He didn't have to wait twenty years; he could get his vengeance now.

"You assholes are going to be serving life," Barrett told him, revelling in the moment.

"Do I know you?" Richard queried, looking like he too had partaken in whatever shit the pile of goo on the bathroom had sunk his nose into.

Where the hell had they got that crap a day out of prison? It didn't matter; they wouldn't be getting any more.

"Whose blood is that?" Richard asked in his aggressively simplistic tone, like a fucking drunk caveman. He looked to Jay on the floor, and the math wasn't adding up.

"Take a guess," Barrett coolly replied. *These assholes are off their face.* He'd been so pumped entering the dilapidated shit-hole, ready to go to fucking war with the hardened cons, and instead they were half cut and offering no real resistance.

Barrett brought the chipped, clawed end of the rusty crowbar down sharply across Richard's nose, instantly shredding the big lump. The nose already looked mangled, but now looked like it'd been shoved through a fucking blender. Richard's hands shot to the middle of his face, covering the sudden explosion of blood, which gave Barrett an opportunity to slam the bar into his ribs, winding him.

Jay started to stir, so rather than continuing to beat the fuck out of Richard, Barrett mounted the larger guy and turned his fucking melon head to paste as he smashed his face into the rotten floorboards. The crowbar vibrated in his hands as he

5

brought it down again and again. Strength was no longer a requirement in the one-sided fight; it was all about stamina.

How long could Barrett last, bringing the steel bar up and down? Cracking bone. Spraying blood and gore. Popping eye balls and flinging gunk which used to serve some kind of function but now painted the shit-stained floor red.

By the time he let up, you wouldn't have known there was a head there in the first place. It looked like someone just ditched a decapitated corpse, because there was no sign of the object that once sat on Jay's thick neck. Just an empty space, with gunky ooze beneath it.

*

Richard hadn't tried to stop the crowbar-wielding maniac. Jay was already dead by the time he'd got his breath back, so saving him wasn't an option. His senses sharpened seeing the disfigured body and adrenaline kicked in, his fight or flight telling him to get the fuck out of there ASAP, especially with a bunch of cracked ribs and a re-broken nose.

Whoever this guy is, I'm no match for him!

He'd taken a couple of wrong turns and was struggling to find the stairs in the rundown apartment building. The place was in disarray, with collapsed walls and blocked corridors. *Ironically condemned.*

The three of them had liked what a fucking maze the shit-hole was when they first arrived. Less chance of being interrupted, or some unannounced parole officer walking in on them. Now he was cursing under his breath at the fucked layout, while crying about his friends' gruesome deaths.

And they were his friends. Yeah, he knew all three of them scumbags. *Low-lifes.* He wasn't immune from the fact. They'd just been in prison for six years for trying to rape a bitch and fucking up some dude…

Fuck! Crowbar dude! That's who he is.

So, yeah, Richard knew what cunts his friends were, but they were *his* cunts. They'd been friends since their days working at the factory together. They'd been through some shit. Been there for each other. He'd been Jay's best man, and helped him though the divorce four months later. They'd gotten Copeland clean in prison and protected him from the multiple beatings he would have otherwise got. They were tight.

But now his best friends were dead. Jay for absolute certain, and judging by the state of the crowbar when that asshole first walked into the room, it was a safe bet Copeland had suffered a similar fate.

"Where the fuck are the stairs?" Richard shouted out in frustration, before covering his mouth like he could take the sound back.

He slipped the hand back to his stinging broken nose but it failed to soften the pain; still, he had to try. He looked round for a weapon but couldn't find anything. The building was ready to fall down but couldn't even provide him with a plank of wood, or a brick. *What the hell.*

No sooner did he finally find the stairs, he was down them, but not by taking them one at a time. His ass was thrown down those unforgiving rickety stairs. His shoulder dislocated as he bounced down the steps and his already busted nose flung blood everywhere. He cracked his elbow against the broken banister and twisted his foot underneath him. He didn't break his ankle, but the sprain would make it harder to get away.

Not that he was going anywhere.

*

Barrett had found the noisy fuck easily enough, shouting

about the stairs he'd just thrown him down.

He followed, being careful with each step he took as the decaying wood groaned beneath him.

It was a mystery how these assholes found this place, but it certainly felt like the exact sort of place they should be. The ugly rundown building matched their cruel personalities and wicked ways.

However, while the building would survive a little longer, Richard and his friends wouldn't. Two were already dead, and the third would soon follow.

Richard managed to open the front door during Barrett's descent but had barely made it past the porch, crawling through a deep puddle while the rain continued its harsh assault. The drains were clogged with takeaway wrappers and cigarette packets. Soggy cartons and shredded newspaper helped the blockage. You could practically see the piss streaming from the sidewalks beneath the graffiti-ridden walls as the murky puddles grew and the paths became rivers. Richard tried splashing through it on pure instinct alone, but made little progress.

Barrett briefly considered dragging the bastard back inside, away from any witnesses, but no-one was out in the rampant storm. If they were, then in all likelihood they were up to no good themselves.

So, instead, Barrett bludgeoned Richard to death in the middle of the waterlogged street, before hauling his ruined carcass to the alley next to the building for another few minutes of dismantling it.

Part of him wished he'd savoured the kills, but after a six year wait, he'd gotten over-excited. Whatever the blue-balls version of wanting to kill a man was, Barrett had it. The second he saw them, he was ready to pop, but he wanted blood, not cum.

He considered pissing over Richard; it would have felt poetic. But the heavy rain would have washed the urine instantly away, joining it with all the other piss in the street.

The important thing was, the three assholes who almost beat him into disability six years ago were now so fucking dead you wouldn't be able to put their pieces back together. *You'd need a vacuum cleaner, not a body bag.*

Barrett smashed the hell out of Richard's body a few more times before disappearing back into the building to fuck the other two corpses up some more. After all, six years was a long wait, and this had all ended far too quickly for them... might as well make a night out of it.

The Morning After Vengeance

The last remnants of the storm had washed most of the three deader than dead scumbags' blood from Barrett by the time he got home.

The streets had still been empty as the rain continued to flood the sidewalks and threaten to go biblical, but eased off just as Barrett turned down his street. *Typical.* He still had a mix and match of skull fragments stuck to his clothes and hair, but he was at least able to walk the several flights of stairs to his apartment without attracting any unwanted attention.

Inside, he bagged the clothes he'd worn, and the crowbar, then hopped in to the shower to scrub away any remaining evidence. He wasn't overly bothered about being caught, but also preferred not to be. If the worst happened, so be it, but he'd take ever precaution to avoid it. After all, they were the assholes who tried to rape a woman and end his life; he just got vengeance.

Don't do the crime if you can't do the time ... *and not the pathetic amount of court appointed time.*

After the shower, Barrett hiked several miles out the damp city with the bag full of clothes and the bloody crowbar. He was someone who always enjoyed a good walk. Sometimes it helped give him time to think, other times he just liked to lose himself in the act. Get away from his problems.

Not that he had any problems this morning; he'd solved them last night with the crowbar. The walks had helped with his recovery too. It was always a good barometer for how close he was to getting back to one-hundred percent.

At the moment, he felt one-hundred percent. He felt fucking great as he took in the post-storm smell which filled the air, and thought about the cold, hard vengeance he'd just dished-out.

Once he'd set the clothes on fire and ditched the crowbar at the bottom of the river, *hopefully never to be discovered*, he wandered back to the city and took his preferred chair by the window in his favourite coffee shop. A long walk and a nice coffee, Barrett's idea of heaven; especially after destroying three degenerates with a crowbar beforehand. *A perfect morning.* He ordered his usual large caramel latte with coconut milk, and sat back in the comfy chair to watch the world go by.

For six years he'd had the image of those three cunts in his mind. Seared into the back of his brain. He'd wake up most days thinking about the assholes, about what they did to him, and what he'd do to them when the opportunity arose. He'd picture them while on the treadmill or therapy table during his recovery. As the doctors, nurses, and physiotherapists pushed his body to the limit to help him rebuild, the sight of those fuckers laying at his feet played on repeat as motivation. They were his true goal. Getting better was important, but it was important in the sense he needed to be fit and healthy to exact his vengeance. To get revenge for everything they'd done to him. To end their miserable pathetic worthless sorry fucking lives! And now he had.

The independent coffeeshop, *The Coffee Home*, was located on a busy street corner offering a view of plenty of traffic and passersby to people watch. It opened early and closed late, and it wasn't uncommon for Barrett to spend a whole day there. He felt like today would be one of those days. He never brought anything to read, and he wasn't one of those regulars with their face buried in a laptop for six hours on just their one coffee. He'd regularly get a fresh brew, sit back, reflect, and watch the world go by.

He was under no illusions comments were probably made about his unusual routine, but he was always polite to the staff and fellow customers. He wouldn't go as far as giving up his favourite spot for an elderly patron, but he wouldn't be rude to anyone either. He just enjoyed the tranquility the familiar place offered. He pondered that the staff must have a nickname for him, or at bare minimum a shortcut description. He never wanted to know what it was; just the idea of it tickled him. *Window Man,* maybe. *They'd change the name if they knew about last night.*

Like everyone who regularly visited the same coffeeshop, Barrett had his favourite barista. Her name was April. She always popped over to say 'hi' during the days he spent there, and often made him fresh coffee and took payment without him having to leave his seat. *No need to worry about someone taking it despite draping his jacket over the chair.* She was polite, friendly, and very pretty. He tried not to leer, but he couldn't help but admire her any chance he got. He knew she'd seen him looking, but was far to kind to make a big deal out of it. It was harmless. Plus, he tipped well.

Today, April had her long chestnut-coloured hair tied up. He always thought she looked extra cute with it up and had mentioned it once. She laughed it off, saying she wore it up whenever she hadn't had a chance to wash it. It didn't change Barrett's mind; he still thought it suited her. He watched her from the corner of his eye a bit longer before turning his attention to the outside world, and thoughts of what next to do with his life.

As he watched the earlier risers walk by, he knew most of them had some idea of how their week would go. They'd be heading to their jobs right now, having a good idea of the day ahead, maybe they'd even know what they'd be having for dinner tonight, what they needed to do with their kids, or how they were going to spend the evening with their other half. He imagined them already thinking about work, or some funny social media post they'd woken up to.

He didn't look down on their routine, there was no judgement on his behalf, but he didn't envy them either. A lot of the time, his life felt like a bore too, but he'd had a defining purpose up until last night.

He'd been consumed thinking about vengeance against those three bastards. That had been his life. His goal, dreams, and ambition, all rolled into one.

But now they were three headless corpses in a neglected building, being fed on by maggots and bugs. Until they were eventually discovered, which he doubted would be anytime soon. It might even be assumed they skipped town before meeting their parole officer. That brought a smile to his face as he contemplated life after vengeance.

A young couple argued outside as they walked passed the coffee shop window. The girl was a few steps ahead, her face bright red with anger, while her loser boyfriend pleaded his case from a few paces behind. Her makeup stained her irate face, and Barrett doubted it had anything to do with the weather. .

He imagined their story: she'd caught him with her best friend, or maybe he'd spent the rent money they didn't have on his poker addiction. Barrett often liked to play this game. Never with the happy couples; there was no fun in that. It was the misery which kept him amused. Got his creative juices flowing.

His thoughts drifted back to his own life as the couple disappeared around the corner. Six years of build up had led to the ultimate release, and he would undoubtedly enjoy it for a long time yet. The euphoric feeling would keep him going for at least the next few months, but afterwards he'd need something new. Something greater. A new purpose.

Something which could surpass the rush he'd felt destroying Copeland, Jay, and Richard. Something to compete with the feeling of turning their heads into mash. Of slamming the crowbar down repeatedly on their prone dead bodies as a rage inside him took over and he let the anger dictate his next move. Something equal to hacking off their limbs, both when they were alive, and dead. *The former was more fun, but both were pleasurable.*

He needed something to fill the void of his addiction to vengeance.

April interrupted his thoughts as she returned to his table during a lull. "Looking tired today," she offered with a beautiful, friendly smile.

"Didn't sleep," Barrett replied, returning the warm gesture, although it looked better on her.

His smile was an awkward one; he didn't use it much, unless he was caving in someone's skull with a crowbar. It wasn't because he was permanently sad or angry; his face just always seemed to be set to neutral. Hard to read, his mother used to say.

"You here for the day?" April asked in a manner which suggested to Barrett she hoped he was.

Barrett knew he wasn't a looker, but something about his conflicting appearance always intrigued people. The broken nose, scars, and shabby hair, gave him an approachable vulnerability rather than scaring people off. On the flip-side, he was always well dressed and looked after his body.

Homeless face and a wealthy body, he often joked to himself. It was like other people found him fascinating, or a mystery which needed to be solved.

He figured it was the case with April too. Plus, what the fuck else was she going to do for her eight hour shift every day? *Why not try and figure out what Window Man's deal was?*

"I think I will be," he eventually replied, adding, "Probably fall asleep in the chair," with a knowing wink to her opening statement.

"Looks like I'll have to keep the coffee and conversation

coming then," she grinned

Just then, a new customer approached the counter and spoiled the flirtatious moment. She turned back to the till as she saw her fellow employee was nowhere to be seen; it was up to her to serve the new arrival.

"Duty calls," she reluctantly told him.

"Fucking customers," Barrett joked, getting an even bigger smile from her.

"Right."

He watched her leave, making sure to take in the sight of her peach ass in the tight black trousers they made all the baristas wear. He wasn't too subtle about it this time around, as the morning was young and only a couple of other people had dared leave the comfort of their homes after the horrendous weather.

Plus, he was sure there was an extra sway in her step which had to be for his benefit, so it would be rude not to look.

Barrett drifted back into his reverie as he watched the world slowly go by through The Coffee Home window while sipping on his sweet flavoured hot drink. He wondered whether now was the time to consider making someone else a part of his life.

A few of the nurses had taken a fancy to him during his long stint in the hospital as they cared for him, and admired his heroics saving the endangered woman from the rapist pigs. He was sure he could contact one of them if he wanted, although the Goldilocks moment had probably passed.

The woman he'd saved had even visited him, and shown more than a fleeting interest after time had passed from the ordeal, but that would have been too weird.

Barrett was used to being alone. He liked it that way. Sure, he'd love a little affection every now and then -- *who wouldn't?* -- but he didn't feel he was built to be around other people long term. He needed his space. Still, it was something to consider as he pondered his next move in life.

He wondered where these thoughts had come from. How had he gone from admiring April's ass, to contemplating settling down, less than half a day after brutally killing and decapitating three men?

Maybe the vengeance was some kind of aphrodisiac? Although it hadn't been in the past.

Maybe he just needed to get laid. To ask April what time she got off work and whether she fancied a drink afterwards. A real drink. Then they could have a fun evening together and maybe go back to his place. He'd joke for a coffee, and draw another beautiful smile from her before he moved in for a kiss. Maybe she'd play her own joke by wearing her hair up for him.

But he didn't want to chance pissing her off and risk his place of sanctuary becoming a hostile environment, or even being banned from it. He doubted it would end up like that -- *how fucking badly would a date have to go for that to be the result?* -- but why take the gamble?

No, what he needed to do was sit back in this preferred spot, drink his favourite drink, admire the gorgeous barista, and relive the memories of last night in his head. Play back the carnage and emotion of ripping them apart with a smile on his face and a skip in his step.

Then, he needed to repeat the process for another few months. Drown himself in the memories daily. Smell the blood, and feel the texture of the skulls as they cracked. Let the vibration of the crowbar reverberate through his body and bring back the imagery of the three of them headless and laying in pools of their own blood. Replay their shock and surprise, their pathetic whimpers and unheard pleas. They hadn't really had a chance to beg for their lives, so sudden were his strikes, but he could add it to the soundtrack. *A little embellishment never hurt.*

Then, he needed to work on putting himself in a position of

having to take a whole new experience of vengeance against some scumbag assholes who would fully deserve the merciless death he'd deliver…

A History Of Vengeance: Part One

Barrett had a long history of taking vengeance. A solid argument could be put forth stating he was addicted to it.

But it didn't start that way. There was nothing in his early childhood which suggested, or caused, such an oddity. He didn't have some drunk piece of shit dad who kicked the fuck out of him, or some bitter abused mum who took out her worldly woes on her young child. There were no missed birthdays or lean Christmases. His parents didn't constantly work double shifts and leave him home alone, or head to the pub every night and tie him to the bedpost with the door locked and his sobs unheard. They loved Barrett, and tried their hardest to give him a wonderful childhood. In return, he loved them too, and was a sweet kid.

Nothing early on hinted at the fact he would later love getting the shit beat out of him. That he'd love to be taken to a near death state in order to recover and set about exacting brutal retribution.

He hadn't known right away how freeing the sensation was, or how it was going to define his entire existence. Once he discovered it, however, there was no turning back.

The love he received in his life wasn't a factor. There would be no psychoanalysing to discover some deep-rooted issue causing this pattern of victim and vigilante. Barrett was simply built differently, and once Pandora's box had been opened, it couldn't be closed.

He was thirteen-years-old when he was on the receiving end of his first real beating. Up until that point, everything had been pretty straight forward barring regularly getting ulcers and not having the greatest grades in school. He wasn't a dumb kid, but wasn't the cleverest either. Average was an overused word to describe many aspects of Barrett's life.

However, he'd soon discover he was way above average in one regard.

*

Scotty Turner was a cunt!

Barrett had always thought so, but largely stayed out of sight of the school bully. Scotty was a big kid for thirteen and used his size to squash anyone in his path. The kid had massive anger issues too and could explode over the slightest thing.

It was the golden rule in Barrett's year: don't piss off Scotty Turner. But sometimes trouble went looking for you.

It was innocuous really; all Barrett did was tackle Scotty while they were playing football in P.E, but it was enough to put Barrett in the bully's crosshairs.

"You're dead meat, Barrett."

That's what Scotty told Barrett after he'd tackled him and passed the ball to Shane Grey.

The whole incident felt like Barrett had committed some great crime against humanity rather than tackling someone while they were playing football. *Isn't that what we're meant to do?* He could hear the gasps from the other kids, like they were watching the crime unfold in slow-motion. They all knew Barrett had done fucked up. The macho P.E teacher - who himself was clearly a former high school bully - always scolded him if he didn't participate; then the one fucking time he did, he got a death threat. *What the fuck!*

For the rest of the day, Barrett's classmates looked at him like he was a dead man walking, and Barrett wondered if he was. He'd seen Scotty Turner fuck up Mikey Hicks behind the bike shed for walking near him in the corridor, and knew how Lee

Wilson took a week off school after getting on Scotty's bad side, only to get a tooth knocked out when he returned. Lee told the teachers he fell over during his lunch break, but everyone saw Scotty punch him in the face while he was eating his sandwich. He'd even stolen the rest of the kids lunch box and tipped it on the floor before making him eat it.

Barrett didn't want to eat his lunch off the dinner hall floor.

A rumour had also spread around the school suggesting the reason Chad Martins left was because he accidentally spilt his orange juice over Scotty and begged his parents to move them all to the other side of the country. Whether there was any truth in the far-fetched hearsay was up for debate, but the point was, you don't fucking cross Scotty Turner, and Barrett had.

Barrett had never been in a fight before; never taken a punch or a slap. He'd never fallen over or broken anything. Rarely even got ill. He'd burnt himself once as a little kid touching a hot pan on the stove, but his mum later told him if she hadn't seen him do it, she wouldn't have had a clue what happened or how he got the mark. Apparently, he'd barely made a sound. A little whimper, rather than a full blown meltdown. She just assumed he was a tough kid, or his brain hadn't registered the pain.

While he was pissed off at having the bully after him, Barrett hadn't been fearful. He hadn't known at that point he could take a punch, and wasn't looking forward to it, but he wasn't shitting his pants like so many other kids suggested he should be. He hadn't considered telling the teachers about the threat -- *you simply don't do that* -- and he wasn't about to make a run for it. He'd quietly accepted his fate, was almost intrigued by it.

Scotty caught up with Barrett outside the school gates and followed him to the field across the road, where he pushed Barrett from behind and stole his schoolbag. Scotty dumped the contents of the bag on the grass before telling Barrett to fight him like a man. The other kids who had followed formed a circle, eager to see the one-sided fight.

Because none of them had any doubt whatsoever, this was going to be a one-sided fight.

Most of the other kids didn't mind Barrett, and he was a pretty tall kid himself for his age, but nothing about him screamed 'chosen one.' He was not going to be the kid who put an end to Scotty Turner's tyrannical reign. If they had been taking bets in the circle, no one would have taken the astronomical odds of Barrett pulling off an upset. A thousand to one would have been a waste of a quid.

Barrett told Scotty to 'fuck off,' which got an 'ooohhhh' from the encircled kids. Scotty response was simplistic: he punched Barrett in the jaw. No pushing or shoving first; just fucking hit him.

Scotty seemed a little shocked, in Barrett's opinion, that he took the punch and remained standing, but Scotty soon landed a second and a third, which did drop Barrett to the muddy grass. Scotty rained down the punches as he mounted him, and Barrett ate them up. The kid's meaty fists slammed down hard on Barrett's face, with some landing on his shoulder as the fucker had zero coordination, but he was big and heavy, and could hit.

Barrett took them all, though. He had wondered what a punch would feel like, and had spent most of the day knowing he was going to be on the receiving end of one.

Now it was happening, it was nowhere near as bad as he expected. Sure, it hurt a little, and he could feel the blood trickling from his nose and a cut forming beneath his eye, but he wasn't out cold seeing cartoon birds. He hadn't puked over himself, or shat his pants.

He put his hands up to defend against the punches -- *that's what you're meant to do* -- but, in all honesty, he was enjoying the beating. Each punch sent a little shiver though his body, akin to the feeling of being on a rollercoaster. It was a thrill. It felt even better than his recent discovery of masturbation.

Where had this feeling had been all his life? Why hadn't the other kids talked about it after Scotty beat them up? Mikey had cried for weeks, while Lee acted like he was getting 'Nam flashbacks anytime anyone brought the incident up. Fuck, Chad and his whole family were in hiding just at the threat of it, if the word around the playground was to be believed; *the latest dumb rumour had them in witness protection.*

Yet, to Barrett, it was a joy. A slightly painful joy, but not something to be scoffed at. Not something to cry about, or be embarrassed by. Something to embrace. It was intoxicating.

Before any more damage could be done to Barrett's face, one of the teachers arrived and broke up the 'fight.' *Someone's going to be in trouble with Scotty for snitching.* Barrett wondered whether they were done. He'd taken his licks, was Scotty satisfied now?

Before he'd even gotten to his feet, Barrett was thinking about revenge. It just popped into his head like it was the next natural step in the process. The evolution of a beating. Take a kicking, recover, then set out to take your vengeance.

It had to be natural, because Barrett was thinking of nothing else. While he'd surprisingly enjoyed being on the receiving end of the bully's assault, he also wanted the thrill of payback. And not just an eye for an eye; something worse.

Barrett smiled as a second teacher helped him to his feet off the muddy ground. They offered him a tissue for his busted nose and walked him back to the on duty nurse at school. They took the smile as him putting on a brave face, not considering for a second the smile was for something a lot more sinister, like vengeance!

Scotty Turner got suspended. Apparently this beatdown was one too many, especially considering the state of Barrett's face in the aftermath. His eyes and cheeks swelled and he looked like he'd stepped out of twelve rounds with a professional boxer.

Barrett's parents demanded action be taken. They thought the little shit who'd done this to their baby boy should be arrested. It never went that far, but he was eventually expelled, and the school assured Barrett's parents it would never happen again, while apologising profusely. Barrett had told his parents it was okay, and to forget about it… but Barrett hadn't forgotten.

Barrett spent the next three months dreaming up ways to hurt Scotty Turner. He let the beating consume him, and it felt euphoric. He'd lay awake rubbing his fingers over the healing wounds and relive the beating blow by blow. He'd play back every heavy, sloppy punch in his head like it was a crowning moment, despite him being on the receiving end.

He'd lost the fight, but felt like the winner. The oafish thug had fucked up his face, but he hadn't really hurt Barrett. He didn't reduce him to tears like all the other kids. Barrett hadn't pleaded and begged for Scotty to stop. In fact, he was pretty certain he'd gained the fucker's respect.

But he didn't want respect… just vengeance.

Enjoying the beating hadn't squashed the rage building inside Barrett. Playing the event over and over threw fuel on the fire. He convinced himself he couldn't get over it until he got payback. That was the end of the story, not survival.

He felt a mixture of happiness and anger as the days passed. He soon learnt, however, that the anger was an extension of the happiness. The anger was all part of the process of vengeance. He took a beating, revelled in it, and was now psyching himself up to dish out retribution. The experience was half complete, left unfinished. He would finish it by fucking destroying Scotty Turner.

Scotty never saw it coming when Barrett struck. Other than the kid's aggressive, abusive, piece-of-no-good-shit father, no-one had ever stood up to Scotty, so he'd become complacent. He never expected for a second any of the kids would set about getting revenge. They'd be fucking stupid to even consider it, let alone try it. He hadn't counted on Barrett.

Barrett jumped him from behind with a dirty tire iron he'd found at a scrap yard, the sort of thing you'd need a tetanus shot for just looking at. He cracked Scotty over the back of the skull with it, dropping him instantly. He laid in several punts afterwards, directed at Scotty's face, busting his nose open just like Scotty had done to him.

Scotty didn't see any of it, just felt it. He begged and pleaded though teary eyes, too busy trying to protect himself to get a good look at his attacker's face. It wouldn't have mattered anyway; Barrett wore a balaclava to keep his identity concealed. He hadn't wanted to, but he had no idea how all this would all go.

Scotty was a blubbering mess by the end of the attack. His face ruined, and his jeans soiled. His reputation in tatters. The giant slain. No kid was going to be scared of someone who pissed themselves mid-beating. The unbeatable, unstoppable, indestructible aura of Scotty Turner was no more.

Barrett enjoyed inflicting the humiliation, and wondered whether he should have pissed himself during his own beatdown. Maybe it wouldn't have been for the best while still at school, but maybe it would have added something even more to the thrilling experience. It certainly seemed to deeply shame Scotty, and therefore excite Barrett.

The rumour mill went wild when word got out the former school bully had been hospitalised. Everyone was a suspect, while at the same time no-one was a suspect. The kids loved the idea of pretending one of them could have done it, but in their minds it had to be a big kid, or an adult. Scotty's dad was the prime suspect, as the incident happened near their home. Others suggested it was a local gang, or high-school kids Scotty had crossed. Still others hinted at it being an older sibling avenging their kid brother. *Piss off enough people, eventually it will catch up with you.*

Barrett didn't so much as get questioned, let alone fingered as a suspect. Was it so inconceivable he could do such a thing? Or a great convenience? Should he be offended no-one for a second believed he was capable of it? Or be happy in his anonymity?

Either way, he felt fucking great. Even his parents seemed happy the kid got the shit kicked out of him. They weren't proud of themselves for feeling that way, but they couldn't deny the smile it brought to their faces either.

Barrett lived off the wave of emotions he took from getting vengeance for months. The beating he received had felt great, but the retaliation was some next level shit, *especially after letting it fester for a while.* Replaying the memories of both worked in harmony, creating some kind of symbolic calm inside him.

It stirred something else deep within, but he was too young to recognise what in the moment.

That would come several years later…

A History Of Vengeance: Part Two

At eighteen, Barrett was jumped by a gang of drunk teens on his way home. He'd already had a long hard night working at the warehouse when the five lads ambushed him in the early hours of the bitterly cold winter morning.

There wasn't any reason for the attack, other than it was late at night, nobody was around, and the group were bored. They leapt on to the road, making Barrett swerve and fall from his bike, then gave him a beating for 'nearly running them over.'

They dragged him to a side street away from the quiet main road and took it in turns punching and kicking him, with each daring the other to be even more vicious than the last. It didn't take long for the punches and kicks to evolve into being tossed against a wall and smashed in the face with a brick.

After that, they ripped the clothes from Barrett's body, leaving him in his boxers, and took it in turns throwing beer bottles at him from afar. They scored points amongst the group based on damage caused, *which was a lot.* The sadistic little fucks were having a great time, the random assault going a long way to curing their boredom.

By the end of the attack, Barrett was a bloody mess. Glass protruded from all over his wrecked, exposed body. His face was shredded with several gashes, some of which would never fully fade. His right ear was badly sliced and required stitches to completely reattach. His nose was broken for the first time and resembled a question mark, *courtesy of the brick to the face.* They'd snapped his ankle with a wild kick, which hadn't registered with Barrett at the time, despite the nasty cracking sound. It became the longest of the injuries to recover from in the aftermath. A few of his fingers had been bent back too which paled in comparison to the other wounds.

And the blood! Scotty Turner had nothing on these guys. They left him in a pool of his own blood. It was lucky he'd rolled to his back at the end of the brutal assault, otherwise he'd have drowned in the mixture of crimson and alcohol. Ironically, the roll did cause even more blood as his bare back crunched against the shattered glass from the broken beer bottles beneath him, but it was better than drowning. There wasn't a part of his body which hadn't been cut; the amount of stitches by the end of the repair job ran easily into the hundreds.

Before the group left, one threatened to set Barrett on fire, seeing as he was soaked in alcohol, *and it was cold out,* but they decided it was crueller to let him live with the face they'd left him. He was spat on by each and left to die, despite them believing it was crueller to let him live.

That part was up to him. Barrett could have crawled to the the main road after they left, but instead chose to continue lying in a pool of his own blood. He lay embracing the immense agony, before the freezing temperatures started to numb the pain. They'd fucked him up good and proper, leaving his body in a state he never previously thought conceivable.

One day, he'd return the favour.

He was found early the next morning by a postman and taken to a nearby hospital, where he spent the majority of the next month as his road to recovery began. Despite getting a good look at every single one of them, he told the police he saw nothing, and didn't remember anything after falling off his bike.

An investigation and appeal for witnesses was launched, but nothing came from it. Not until eighteen months later... which was how long Barrett waited for his vengeance.

He'd spent a lot of time in his bedroom over the course of his recuperation. The same room where he'd spent hours dreaming up ways of hurting Scotty Turner was now a haven for planning vengeance on the wicked gang who left him for dead.

Barring the interruptions from his doting parents, *making sure he was comfortable,* Barrett's thoughts churned with ideas and questions of how far he was willing to go to exact his vengeance. Should he replicate what they did to him? Or go much much further?

The idea of killing someone wasn't something Barrett had given much heed to previously, but the notion stuck in his head the moment they threatened to burn him alive.

That was the first time he'd truly been scared. The idea they could have gone unpunished by him if they'd killed him brought Barrett the closest he'd ever come to crying. The pain and shame of the attack *needed* to be followed with the glow of vengeance. It was a symbiotic relationship. It's what made Barrett whole. Nothing less would do.

Thinking about it made Barrett realise he'd never dwelled on what happened to Scotty after his retaliation. He could have killed Scotty that day, and other than the concern of being caught, it wouldn't have mattered. He never checked on how Scotty's life had been affected afterward. Whether it'd profoundly changed him as a person in any way. Whether Scotty had suffered any permanent physical damage from the attack, which handicapped his day to day life. He hadn't gloated about the victorious assault, or confided in anyone what he'd done. He took his vengeance, absorbed the happiness it brought him, then moved on. If he had killed Scotty at the time, *or if Scotty succumbed to the injuries after,* it wouldn't have made the slightest difference to Barrett.

If this vengeance was to be the same, then why shouldn't he just fucking end them?

He discovered the group of lads were part of a local gang.

After finding out about their hideout, he barricaded all the doors and set the building ablaze with them all trapped inside.

In total, nine people died that night, seven male and two female, in what was considered a gang-related incident. None of them knew why they'd died, which, unlike Scotty Turner never knowing who beat the fuck out of him, bothered Barrett.

He wished they had at least peered through a window as they melted and sizzled; caught sight of him as their skin charred and their lives went up in flames. They should've known who the author of their fate was, after what they'd done to him.

That would have been the cherry on top.

*

Between the attack, recovery, and vengeance, the whole ordeal lasted eighteen months; and they were by far and away the best eighteen months of Barrett's life. The best time, in fact, since the whole Scotty Turner incident.

It was at this point Barrett began to truly realise the profound effect the attacks, recovery, and subsequent vengeance had on him. The euphoric feeling which ran through his body during all three stages. How each brought a different joy.

He felt at peace during the vicious assaults. Centered. Like the world suddenly made sense. His high pain threshold dulled the punches and kicks, which in turn heightened his awareness, allowing him to fully soak up what was happening. The beauty in the violence.

It permitted him to be at one with himself, and the world, as pleasure and pain formed an unbreakable bond. He was in tune with God and the Devil. *The stars were aligned, and all the rest of that bollocks.*

Barrett couldn't explain it, but he knew getting the fucking shit kicked out of him was his happy place. He didn't want to water down the liberating sensation by experiencing it every day, but he craved it.

Then there was the recovery. The healing process brought its own whirlwind of strong emotions. Barrett loved to let the beatdown fester in his mind. Eat away at him. Make him angry, frustrated, filled with hate. It added a layer of torture to the already excruciating uncertainty of whether he'd be able to walk right ever again, or the nausea he felt seeing his fucked up face in the mirror during those early days when everything was still puffy, bruised, and broken. When he didn't even recognise who he was looking at.

Deep inside, however, he was smiling. He knew retribution was coming. But until then, he basked in the feeling of helplessness, and the concern shown by others. The sympathy from his parents. The empathy from all those around him who tried to put him back together again. He lived for the triumphs and successes of regaining his ability to walk, rebuilding his strength, and watching his wounds heal. There was something incredibly empowering about it all. The whole process was fascinating. All the while, he'd think about vengeance, the grand prize.

Despite it being the most satisfying component, it was the part Barrett hadn't perfected yet. Vengeance.

His revenge on Scotty Turner had been truly incredible, an orgasmic experience the likes of which no sex could ever compare. Life-changing. He'd experienced some of the joy again when burning the gang alive, but it hadn't come close to reaching the intoxicating levels of Scotty. He'd wondered whether taking a life would add something special to the process -- *even more so when he found out he'd taken nine lives* -- but arson had lacked the personal touch.

He couldn't judge whether killing had enhanced the

vengeance or not. What he did know was he needed to do it up close and personal. To see their lives taken. To have the cause of it in his hand. A canister of gasoline and a box matches didn't count. The tire iron he used to wreck Scotty felt more natural. More organic. He missed that connection. Barrett knew the next time he took vengeance on someone who'd wronged him, he'd make it more intimate. More personal.

No links were made between the people who died in the fire and those who put Barrett in hospital. He wasn't spotted or identified as being in the area, and therefore was never questioned for the crime. Having also never described the people who attacked him, no-one was likely to ever put the pieces together. In the eyes of the law, Barrett had nothing to do with the arson, and he was never considered a suspect.

It didn't bother Barrett either way; as far as he was concerned, *he'd done the world a fucking favour.*

*

The third attack came two years after the fire, but it was the first time Barrett had manipulated the situation, putting himself in a position for it to happen.

He visited a rough pub in a bad area, the very definition of wrong side of the tracks, which was even the name of the pub. There, he made a pass at a girl belonging to one of the two local hard-cases, knowing it would cause him a world of hurt. The brutes both had a reputation for striking first and asking questions later. Not that any answer Barrett could give would exonerate him from the crime of all crimes: moving in on one of their women.

Barrett had fallen into a full belt of depression following the unexpected death of his parents. A car crash. They hit a patch of ice, spun from the road and collided with a tree. It was deemed an accident, no one's fault, and therefore no one to blame or retaliate against. The grief of losing them hit Barrett hard, but the feelings weren't the same as what he felt when he set about getting vengeance.

Something he once again craved, and for the first time, felt he truly needed. He was struggling for any kind of fulfilment and happiness as he adjusted to life without them.

The combination of the money they'd left him -- even after the ridiculous inheritance tax -- and of selling the family home to move into a tiny flat meant he was comfortable financially. He only worked his dead-end job to pass the time while he found his feet. A purpose.

That purpose came when the two meatheads took offence to Barrett's advances on one of their girls, and put him in a fucking coma.

It's not like he had been inappropriate to the lady; Barrett was always respectful. But the very notion of flirting with her while those two gorillas were in the pub was blasphemous.

One, "Oi, asshole, that's my bird you're speaking to," later, and Barrett had a pool cue broken across his skull, then was slammed into the pool table so hard he didn't wake up for two months.

The police were dumbfounded by Barrett's luck when they looked back at his file. The incident with Scotty was no longer on record, but being jumped twice was some shitty misfortune. Barrett agreed, and had to refrain from smiling. They were baffled by his choice of pub, given he didn't seem like a fucking degenerate asshole -- *the type they normally associated with the establishment* -- but Barrett claimed he hadn't known what he was walking into.

Whether they bought it or not didn't matter; Barrett was the victim here.

The whole experience had turned out very different this time around. There had been no immense, almost spiritual, gratification while being on the receiving end of the beating, because it was over as quickly as it started. Barrett had always relied on his high pain threshold to prolong the smackdown and enjoy the thrill of getting his ass kicked, but they'd put him in a coma as soon as the fight started. He wasn't even sure if he'd ever been knocked out properly before, but those two skinheads achieved it in record time.

Then the initial aftermath was robbed from him too. He had all kinds of fucked up dreams and imagery in his coma, but it wasn't the same as stewing on the thoughts while his body began to heal. He couldn't replay the fight over and over in his head like he had the last two times. Let it torment him and increase his thirst for vengeance.

Instead, his dream like state dictated what he saw. Most of it was some kind of fucked up negotiation for his soul with the Devil; about surviving this ordeal so he could take the very vengeance he so dearly sought. It was all very abstract and odd, but it kept his brain ticking over until he woke.

Barrett had always considered himself invincible, due to his high tolerance and outstanding recovery ability. He always survived, and bounced back. Awaking from a coma was the ultimate test of that, and making a full recovery -- *barring some minor brain damage and constant headaches* -- was proof he was unbreakable. Not in the Bruce Willis sense; as he knew he could be hurt, but he certainly considered himself closer to a superhero than a regular Joe.

The two skinhead fuck-faces who put Barrett in a coma were called Billy and Danny. Both had skipped town on the night of the brawl, believing they'd killed Barrett. Which, according to the doctors, they had, albeit only briefly as he was resuscitated on site.

Barrett was constantly told he was lucky to be alive, and should see this as a new opportunity in life, but he didn't believe it was luck. He believed it was his own toughness and determination. His own invincibility. His strong will for vengeance, something he would be getting whether those two fuckers skipped town or not.

It took him a little over half a year after his recovery to find Billy and Danny. He carefully followed leads through their friends and family, including the woman he'd flirted with to put himself in this mess, and eventually tracked them down.

Life hadn't treated either of them well since the attempted murder. Both had to lay low, and struggled with risky cash-in-hand jobs via connections with some very shady characters. They'd fallen in with the wrong people and were no longer the toughest guys in town. Instead, they were grunts for others. *Bitches*, although neither would admit to that. Both might have considered turning themselves in and doing the reduced time if they'd known Barrett was alive, but they didn't find that out until he caught up with them.

There wouldn't be any jumping from behind or burning buildings this time, as Barrett tried the torture route.

After successfully drugging and kidnapping the men, he kept them in a dingy basement, brutalising them every day while listening to their pathetic pleas. The first two days, they'd begged for their freedom, but by the third night they were praying for death. *Amazing what a botched castration could achieve.*

He regularly went to town on them both with a crowbar, which he had decided was his new weapon of choice. It felt good in his hand, and caused a lot of damage. The clawed end gave it a bigger Swiss Army knife appeal too, as he alternated which part of the crowbar he used.

Barrett broke most of their bones over the course of a week. He plucked out an eye each, and even considered some mad-scientist swapping of the eyeballs with a glue gun, but the thought was funnier in his head than the effort of doing it. *Plus, it wasn't really his style.*

He ripped every tendon, shredded every muscle, and tore away plenty of skin. He kept them alive the best he could while he continued the torture, but eventually they both succumbed, leaving Barrett to pulverise what remained until no more satisfaction could be gained.

In hindsight, the torture approach wasn't quite for him. He enjoyed elements of it, but didn't get his thrills from screams and begging. He preferred sudden brutal violence and instant gratification when it came to the taking of vengeance. Kidnapping them had been the best part; the initial buzz of action hit all the right spots. Lit up the endorphins.

After that, though, he was only going through the motions, as the outcome had already been determined.

That's not to say he didn't have fun, because he did, but it lacked the immediate satisfaction he got from beating the fuck out of Scotty in the moment.

He was closer to perfecting his vengeance formula, but wasn't quite there yet.

*

The incident with the attempted rapists, and his branding as a saviour, would be the next and last time Barrett was assaulted. It took him longer to exact his vengeance, due to them ending up in prison first, but when it did arrive, Barrett felt the formula had been perfected.

Ferociously taking them out head on with the crowbar and spending the night hacking up their pieces and smashing their face to salt was the ultimate high. The euphoric state he'd been looking to recapture. The joyous feeling would linger with him for a long time, but he wasn't done yet. Not by a long shot.

Life After Vengeance

Life took several twists and turns for Barrett after disposing of the three would-be rapists.

He never did ask April out, and once again found himself moving cities to start afresh. He still had plenty of money from the sale of his parents' house, their will, and various injury claims for the beatings he'd taken, but he made sure to work regularly and keep his mind focused. He tried his hand at everything from factory work to office work. He didn't really have a face for working retail -- *something he was more self-conscious about than others* -- but it never appealed anyway. He went through jobs quickly, but never departed on bad terms. He was just eager to try something different.

Barrett kept himself fit and healthy, and soon found a new coffeeshop to relax in, and a new barista to admire. He watched the world go by and continued making up stories for the less happy couples and loners walking the streets. He carried on suffering regular headaches, and once again often found himself with a mouth full of ulcers, like he had as a kid. He never did anything to ease either as he couldn't help but enjoy the discomfort they caused.

He started trying to date but never really clicked with anyone, and ended up sampling a few hookers instead. They were all kind to him, but sex had never been Barrett's strong point. He could tell they were bored. He didn't have an ego when it came to defending his masculinity; he just wanted a little contact, which they delivered, so their boredom never bothered him. Barrett soon lost interest in sex and relationships, having had his pick-me-up dose of affection.

Thoughts of vengeance flickered into his mind from time to

time but it was too soon to try again, and he was still getting mileage from the last lot taken. He occasionally looked for other pleasures to fill the gap as an alternative but nothing ever quite hit the spot.

Any kind of competitive fighting lacked the danger, and if he let himself become a punching bag a ref or trainer would jump in fearing he was getting hurt. *Which was the point.* Cutting himself didn't take, nor did any thrill-seeking adventures like bungee-jumping or skydiving. No kink in the bedroom brought the desired results either, not that he had much of a chance to try. He wasn't the sort to get into random brawls for a quick fix, nor did he want to take any vengeance which wasn't meaningful.

He laughed at the pretentiousness of that thought, but it was the truth. He never wanted to sully the true meaning of his life. A hole was starting to form in the absence of new vengeance, but Barrett knew it wasn't time to fill it yet.

*

A year after his last vengeance, Barrett got himself a job in construction, and a few months later met a girl, Alice. The two hit it off right away. She was unperturbed by the faded scars on his face, or his crooked nose, and had no issue with his lack of skills in the bedroom. If anything, she found it adorable, and set about improving his technique. Alice was a theatre actress, a fair few years younger than Barrett, a shy woman who came into her own whenever she was performing on stage, *or in the bedroom.*

The two met at the coffeeshop Barrett regularly visited. She was intrigued by this stoic man being there all the time, and he'd noticed her plenty ... even more so than Carmen the coffee-filler, as he'd dubbed the slightly plump and extremely pretty barista he had a thing for.

Alice's reason for being there were because she liked the background noise while she learnt her lines. Which seemed a much more substantial reason than his, 'I've got nothing else to do,' but the remark did work as a good icebreaker.

They saw each other a few times a week after that, and it wasn't long before he was attending all her shows, and meeting her co-stars while being regarded as her boyfriend. Barrett always considered Alice way too beautiful for him, and could only imagine what some of her more handsome stuck-up co-stars thought, but he never doubted Alice's fondness for him. Despite her good acting skills, Barrett always knew where he stood with her. He became the love of her life, and she told him so plenty. He couldn't help but return in kind, and meant it too.

The two of them married less than a year after meeting. It wasn't part of Barrett's plan in life to ever get married, wasn't even something he'd considered -- *or in all honesty thought possible* -- but you never knew where life was going to take you. Nine months after marrying they had a kid together, a baby girl they named Jade.

Months and years passed as Barrett built a life for himself and his family. He made a fantastic father, and was a loving husband. He provided for his family the best he could and adored their time together. They brought a house, and Barrett eventually started his own business after gaining enough experience within his construction work.

Any thoughts of vengeance had left his mind; instead his days were filled with laughter and happiness as he watched his little pride and joy grow.

Even when another kid pushed his young daughter over, causing her to need stitches in her right knee, Barrett didn't consider getting vengeance on the youngster. If anything, Alice was more full of hellfire than him.

He may have secretly wished Jade sought vengeance herself,

but it wasn't a lesson he'd teach her, just like his parents never suggested such a thing to him after the whole Scotty Turner thing. He had a sweet kid who reminded him of himself in a lot of ways -- *while thankfully looking like her mother* -- and he didn't want to corrupt that.

In the early days of his business, a few clients decided to fuck him over causing Barrett to lose a fair bit of money, but once again he refrained from any kind of vengeance. It would have had a different feel to it anyway, being more betrayed than physically harmed, but the old him would have still looked for some kind of retribution. He would have found a way to suffer the physical pain, like confronting the bullying clients in private and hoping they reacted violently. Instead, Barrett took it on the chin. Was the better man, albeit a couple of thousand pounds down because of it.

Alice never knew about his vengeance, or the fact he'd killed fourteen people. He'd told her about being jumped by the gang, being put in a coma by the thugs at the pub, and rescuing the woman from being raped, but never filled her in on the ends of those stories. As far she she was concerned, they were still somewhere out in the world, hopefully serving time. He gave Alice the background story of each and every scar staining his body, and never once had to lie. He'd never suffered an injury while getting justice, each scar was on record, and none were his fault.

Barrett never looked back on any of the beatings or vengeance with regret. He took great pride in each and every one of them, even if he couldn't show it. The scars reminded him of some of the best moments in his life. The only regret he had was his beautiful bride and lovely young daughter would never get to meet his parents. His mum and dad would never get to meet the sweet granddaughter they'd probably doubted they'd ever have. He'd shown Jade pictures of them, and told stories of their kindness, but it wasn't the same. Jade even named her favourite stuffed rabbit Susan after Barrett told her it was her grandma's name.

In that moment, vengeance was the furthest thing from his once again beating heart.

As with everything in life, there were some ups and downs along the way. Some self doubt, and tough choices, the normal obstacles thrown at you. Money problems, health scares, the stress of day to day life, those sort of things, but the three of them always stuck together. *Us against the world.*

Alice started doing the accounts for Barrett's growing business as the acting jobs dried up, and they managed a good balance of work and home life always finding a way to separate the two. For the first time in Barrett's life he went abroad as well, having previously only ever holidayed in the UK due to his father's irrational fear of flying.

The three of them visited various islands in Europe over the years as family holidays. Lying beaten and broken in hospital beds, uncertain as to whether he'd be able to walk again, became replaced with long walks on sandy beaches and drives up picturesque mountains. Poolside cocktails and getting a tan replaced IV tubes and pain killers. The thrill of getting the hell kicked out of him faded as the excitement of what adventure they'd go on next as a family was brought to the foreground. His previous bliss was reframed. Seeing the joy his daughter felt over every little thing which made her smile became his new happy place.

Sex with his loving wife may not have competed with the exhilaration of shattered bones, but it wasn't a nothing sensation either. Her touch lit him up in ways he hadn't previously felt. The caress of her fingers along his body felt equal to a punch in the face. Brought a similar joy. Being inside her was akin to the glass cutting his cheek as the gang bottled him, or him burning them alive for their sins. It was a joy he hadn't known he'd ever feel again, yet here it was. The pain was replaced by pleasure, but the end thrill was similar. He'd always seen the two sensations as bring similar, and he'd been right; now they were just flipped with pleasure being the dominant feeling. Nothing could fully recreate the broken bones and festering revenge lingering in his mind after an attack, nor the heavenly bliss of exacting savage vengeance as he killed those motherfuckers who'd wronged him, but he didn't need it anymore. He'd found a suitable substitute, and one which was healthier for him in the long run.

Life was good.

*

The weather was foul on the drive home from the airport after their latest holiday. The rain battered the windscreen and the wind howled outside the car like it was roaring to get in. It had been a rocky, somewhat scary, landing as the plane touched down on the runway reminding Barrett of why his own father had been so adamant about not flying.

If God wanted us to fly, he'd have given us wings. Barrett smiled at the faint memory.

The shaky landing had also brought their holiday officially to an end, and day to day life was set to restart. *The worse part of any trip away.* Two weeks in Tenerife had been just the break Barrett and Alice needed from work, even if they were always reluctant to take time off, while their fourteen year old daughter Jade was never going to say no to sun and sand. The girl would live on a beach if she could.

But now they were back, and the weather was making that abruptly clear. Sun and sandals to rain and coats in the space of one flight home. Jade sat in the back of the car fighting the feeling of tiredness as she texted her friends during the drive, while Alice was mentally preparing what needed to be done in the morning after a nice long lie-in. They'd landed late in the evening and wouldn't make it home much before midnight, but could only afford themselves one more day off at most. Barrett was already planning on doing some light work tomorrow morning and maybe getting back into the swing of things by the afternoon.

Work had been going well over the years and the business had grown nicely. Alice had been a godsend with the accounts, having some kind of natural aptitude for it. He'd taken on several other employees, and was even training one of them up to be his successor when the time was right, and he could allow himself early retirement. That was still many years away, but was already something Barrett and Alice thought about. Gone was the need to have a job to occupy his mind, Barrett was more accustomed to enjoying the little things in life.

He was sure he'd get some shit from his employees about his bright red 'tan.' Lord knows Jade had laughed about it enough. While Alice and Jade tanned like goddesses, Barrett was never built for anything other than the doom and gloom of British weather, although it hadn't stopped him chilling on the beach. No matter how many of these holidays they went on, he still always forgot to wear suncream for the first few days despite Alice always offering it. She thought he was a masochist. *If only she knew.*

Alice held Barrett's knee on the drive all the way home. Down the years her affection for him had only grown. While other couples may have drifted with age, they'd become closer. She may have initially been intrigued by his stoic nature, but chiselling it away over the years and bringing out a more light-hearted version of him had filled her with even more joy. Barrett stole a glance at her every chance he got, her tanned toned body radiant after the fun in the sun. She was more beautiful every day in his eyes.

How'd I get so lucky?

They arrived home just after midnight with the rain and strong wind still not relenting. Maybe not quite a storm of the century, but not fun to come home to either. Barrett was tempted to leave the suitcases in the car but wanted them safely inside the home; plus they had bits they'd need. He grabbed Alice and his case, while a sleepy Jade took her own, moaning about the wind and needing to pee.

Alice fumbled with the keys in her own tired manner before unlocking the front door and announcing to herself she was 'home sweet home.'

A gloved hand wrapped around her mouth just as she noticed the broken kitchen window down the hallway.

Addicted To Vengeance

Barrett hurried Jade towards the house, locking the car door as the howling wind picked up and the sheets of rain battered them. He needed her out of the dire weather as she started shivering and the temperature dropped a notch.

When they bundled the suitcases inside Barrett switched the light on -- *which for some reason Alice hadn't already* -- and a wooden club connected with the side of his head. The impact dropped him to his knees. A dull pain reverberated round his body, releasing endorphin, and making Barrett feel like an ex-smoker sucking on his first cigarette in years.

Man, it tasted good. But what the fuck?

Four men, all wearing black with their faces covered, stood around him. One had a tight grip on Alice. A skull tattoo with roses in the empty eye sockets peeked from his wrist as he wrapped his hand around her throat. He wasn't choking her with his large hands, more warning Barrett not to try anything stupid. If further incentive was required, another of the intruders pointed a gun at Jade's head as he held her against his body. While his face was covered with a balaclava, his mouth wasn't, and Barrett saw him lick his lips at the closeness. All very intentional as he eyeballed Barrett.

The remaining two held baseball bats and bin liners filled to the brim with what Barrett assumed was their stuff. Another couple of bags sat on the floor next to the group, also overflowing with everything they'd been able to snatch.

They'd walked in on a burglary, and the four men didn't look happy about it.

"Give us your keys and your fucking wallet," the leader of the four demanded in a gruff voice as he held Barrett's daughter. It was the type of voice which had done a fifteen-year stint somewhere.

He pressed the gun harder against Jade's temple, making her yelp as a fresh wave of fear struck when the texture of the barrel scraped against her skin. Urine drizzled down her skinny jeans. She'd held it in the whole journey home but, the gun loosened the resistance.

"Daddy," she cried, pleading for him to help.

"Take it easy," Barrett said as he removed the wallet from his pocket; he handed it over, along with the car keys. "Don't hurt her," he added as he sized the four men up.

The one holding the gun to his daughter was the biggest. Barrett could see his muscles bulging through his black clothes. The one restraining Alice wasn't far behind -- *probably gym buddies.* The other two were slightly shorter, but still as tall as Barrett and much wider than him.

These men meant business.

"You're in no position to negotiate," the thug holding Alice barked at him. He redirected his attention to his prisoner. "What about you, bitch? you got a purse tucked into those tight jeans?"

He stuffed his hand into her empty pocket and grabbed hold of her thigh which sent a shiver up Alice's spine. He could feel her repulsed reaction as he held her; it brought a smile to his cruel lips. He couldn't help but lick the side of her face to wind the whore up further. She tried to struggle, but he was in control.

"Just take the stuff and leave. We don't want any problems," Barrett bargained.

"What'd we say about negotiating?" the gun wielding leader replied.

"You're the dumb fucks who walked in on us. This is on you, not us," the smaller of the two bag carriers told Barrett. He let out a horrible snort as he spoke, like he wasn't sure if he was angry, or telling a joke, and got caught somewhere in the middle. It was disgusting.

Barrett could see the shape of his laptop pointing from the bottom of the bag the snorter held. Fuck knows what else these assholes had taken, but he suspected it was everything. They were insured, but what a pain in the ass. For the moment, he just wanted them out of his house and away from his family; he could deal with everything else later.

The leader noticed the piss dripping down Jade's leg, and against his own.

"This little bitch pissed over me," he proclaimed, tossing Jade to the floor with the gun still aimed at her. "Need your fucking diaper changed love," he sneered as he tugged at her wet jeans.

Before Barrett could react to the escalation, both the bag carriers dropped the stolen goods and began laying into him with their bats. It had been a long time since Barrett had tasted his own blood as the bat cracked across his mouth, busting his lip and loosening some teeth. He fell to the ground, trying to protect himself, while at the same time basking in the memory of former beatings.

Each vicious swing from the bats felt like it rebooted something inside him. Jump-started memories long since abandoned. A bash to his right shoulder reminded him of the sloppy but powerful punches that dickhead Scotty Turner gave him in his first ever beating. He hadn't thought about the bullying asshole in ages. A crack which busted his jaw took him back to the alley and the beer bottles being thrown at him, while a blast of the wooden bat to the back of his skull quickly jolted the memory of being put in a coma.

That one hurt! It still wasn't the level of pain any normal man would feel, but Barrett noticed he was a little more sensitive there than anywhere else.

Another blow of the bat, colliding with his nose, had

Barrett's mind recalling the would-be rapists he'd crushed all those years ago. This time he was remembering the pain he inflicted on them rather than his own.

They didn't ease off with the onslaught, as they made sure Barrett got the picture that he was fucking helpless to make the save. *They were in control.* The bats continued to connect, and Barrett continued to absorb the blows with his head face down against the floor as the wood crunched against his body. His hands protected the back of his head like he was under arrest, but everything else was fair game as they continued to swing.

He was sure they were trash talking him but he couldn't hear the words above the noises his wife and daughter were making as they pleaded for the attackers to leave him alone, and to get the fuck off of them.

Barrett could see from the corner of his eye Alice screaming and kicking as the muscular prowler held her; it only seemed to excite him. He knocked Alice to the floor, landing her side-by-side with their traumatised daughter as each was straddled by their respective captors. Alice carried on fighting, much to the soon-to-be rapist's amusement. He tried yanking the clothes from her body as she continued to struggle.

One of the bat swingers briefly left Barrett and whacked Alice across the head with the blood-stained bat. It occurred to Barrett it must be his blood as he watched the asshole do an unusual out-of-place jig after smashing her with the bat. *The cunt thinks he's in Clockwork Orange.*

"That'll learn you," the dancing asshole joked, as he joined in tearing Alice's clothes from her back with a hopeful glint in his eyes, praying he'd get some sloppy seconds. The blow rocked Alice and made it easier for them to finish stripping her as the man with the tattoo dropped his own trousers, ready for a bit of the old in-out.

Barrett's attention drifted to the guy with the gun as he

watched him slide the barrel of the weapon across his daughter's belly, threatening to make a new hole. Her tears only increased, much to the scumbag's amusement. He settled the unfired gun down instead and penetrated her with his crooked veiny cock, in unison with Skull Tattoo jamming his hard thick rod deep inside Alice's dry pussy.

Both women let out pained anguished yelps as the double violation began. Alice's tears for her own intrusion were nothing compared to those she felt for her daughter. The pure terror and excessive hurt on Jade face would be etched into Alice's mind forever. She *had* to save her daughter, no matter the cost.

Alice smashed her fists again her rapist's chest, trying to dislodge him, but he barely noticed. Her punches were weak as her eyes started to roll back in her head from the aftereffects of the baseball bat and the agony of the brutal rape. She wanted to fight back, to save herself, and more importantly her daughter, but her attempts were barely getting his attention, let alone stopping him. She wanted to bite him, but he held her down. She wanted to claw his fucking eyes out, but he bent her arms underneath her. She wanted to knee him in the nuts but her legs were pinned. Everything she tried was useless, but she couldn't give up.

The rapist started to speed up now he had full control of her. He dug his fingers into her shoulder blades and took a firmer grip as he rammed down on her harder and harder. His fat cock churned up her insides as he smashed her with reckless abandonment. Each powerful thrust looked like he was trying to snap the woman in half. *A few more like that and he just might.* He was having the time of his life.

And to think, they'd only come here to steal some shit.

Barrett felt the room spinning from the blow to the back of the head as he watched his wife and daughter both being violently raped.

His daughter's screams were muffled as the possible ex-con grabbed her mouth and squeezed it shut while he continued to pump away. His other hand groped her small tits as he slobbered over her neck and licked the side of her face like a hungry wolf ready to devour its prey. The look on her face was one of unimaginable fright, the likes of which Barrett had only ever seen on his own victims before he started tearing off limbs.

The baseball bat pair assumed they'd done a number on Barrett, but the years hadn't softened him. He could still take a fucking beating and keep on ticking. His pain threshold was still dialled up to the max. Barrett could feel the warmth of the blood around his mouth. His ears were ringing, his nose re-broken, and some bones may well have been snapped.

Despite it all, and the accompanying disorientation from the blow to the back of his head, he was certain he could make it to his feet and fight the intruders off. Or, at bare minimum, he could make enough noise to alert the neighbours, if they hadn't been already. Maybe he could chase these cunts off, at least get them away from his wife and daughter. But…

… he didn't try…

… Instead, he watched.

He soaked up the agony on his sweet daughter's face. The lost of her innocence and virginity all in one go. He watched as she suffered the first true terror of her life, and wondered whether she'd respond to the brutal assault the same way he had all those years ago. Whether he'd passed the yearning on to her. Would she have the same thirst for vengeance he did? He pictured the two of them setting off side-by-side in the future to hunt these savage fuckers down and absolutely annihilate them.

A family outing, like the holiday they'd just been on.

He wondered whether his wife would join them. He couldn't have passed it on to her, but he was sure she would feel the same. That she'd want these cunts dead after what they did to their little girl. Alice always had fire in her eyes when she was pissed off; it was one of the things he fell in love with, the anger she could conjure when needed. The shy woman who wasn't to be crossed. It was never unjust, nor would it be this time, aimed at the bastards who raped her, and their child. Barrett could definitely picture her standing alongside Jade and him. The three of them together, addicted to vengeance.

Alice bucked the tattooed asshole off her as he came. Half his juice splashed against her inner thigh, while the rest squirted inside her. She clawed at the eyes of the man next to her as her arms were released, getting him off her petrified daughter rather than worrying about her own attacker, who was still enjoying some post-orgasmic bliss.

Climbing to her feet, Alice kicked the leader in the face, fully knocking him off Jade. She picked her daughter up from the floor and ran with her to the kitchen. The other invaders fumbled over their fallen comrade as they chased after them.

Alice screamed for Barrett to help as she grabbed the biggest knife she could find from the block on the kitchen side and positioned Jade behind her. The fire in her eyes was there in abundance.

It was exactly how Barrett imagined she'd look taking her vengeance. *I know my wife well.* He wondered whether his eyes looked like that when he'd pulverised those men, or burnt the building down with the gang inside. He'd never seen himself taking vengeance; this was the closest he'd come to seeing the act in third person.

He looked to his daughter, cowering behind his fierce wife. Tears dripped from her shocked face as her small hands clutched her bleeding vagina. There was nothing but torment in her eyes. She wasn't thinking about revenge, or fucking killing these cunts, she was struggling to breathe. She was scarred, broken, damaged beyond repair. Her life had just been emphatically changed forever and she wasn't sure how to cope with it. She began to hyperventilate, knowing the cruelty wasn't over yet as the four men closed in. Alice rested a hand on Jade's shoulder trying to offer some small act of comfort, but there wasn't any to be had.

The four intruders circled Alice as she implored Barrett to get up and help. She could see he'd taken a brutal beating, but his eyes were open, and if she could fight back, her man could too. He'd never shown any aggression in their time together, but she'd seen his ripped and scarred torso everyday for the last fifteen years. She'd seen him work on building sites and not break a sweat. Her man was a beast. A wolf in sheep's clothing. She needed him to show that side.

Little did she know, he was....

Barrett had a choice to make. Get the fuck up and and help his wife and daughter, or... let it play out, and later down the line hunt these bastards down and make them suffer on a biblical level.

He hadn't thought about vengeance in a long time, and hadn't missed it. The hole in his life had been replaced by the love of his wife and daughter, but lying on the floor watching the carnage unfold, it was all coming back to him.

The pain he was feeling was unrivalled. He'd always had an unnaturally high tolerance to physical pain, but the emotional pain he was going through watching his family suffer at the hands of these sadistic animals was a sensation he never thought feasible.

The hurt they'd caused *him* was some next level shit. He could feel real tears in his eyes, genuine anguish in his vulnerable heart. They'd broken a vital piece of him, and not just a bone. It felt phenomenal!

Where has this feeling been all my life?

He could only briefly wallow in the new feeling as he watched his wife stab the knife at the asshole who'd held a gun to their daughter's head before raping her. The gun which was now left unguarded, mere feet away from Barrett. He had no intention of using it however, despite his wife's screeching pleas and his daughter's abundance of heartbroken tears. The leader snatched the knife easily away from Alice, and turned it back on her.

Barrett committed to memory the look of betrayal in his wife's eyes as the man plunged the knife deep into her belly, while he hadn't moved a muscle to stop it. She looked to Barrett as she fell to the tiles clutching her punctured bloody stomach. 'Why didn't you help us,' was clearly etched across her face, even if she couldn't get the words out.

Instead, she mumbled something about 'my baby,' while losing the battle to keep the blood pouring from her carved stomach as the maniac with the knife stabbed her three more times. She fell on top of Jade in one last desperate act to protect her from the circling monsters as blood gushed to the kitchen floor and her life began to fade.

Barrett knew Alice couldn't believe he hadn't saved her, and for that, he was sorry. She'd expected him to spring into action the whole time and rip these motherfuckers apart, and he hadn't. He would do that for her, but not yet.

He needed to let it simmer first. He needed to let the assault torment him for a year or two before he went looking for them.

What he felt in this moment was too big to act on right away. It needed to be savoured, even if it cost him his wife's life. The vengeance he'd take for this would be unlike anything ever dreamt up before.

In time, those bastards would get it worse than any man who ever lived. He silently promised Alice that as she took her last breath. Whatever her thoughts, or feelings of betrayal, he'd avenge her. He'd avenge both of them.

Alice didn't know that, and would never have accepted it even if she did. She'd needed him. *They'd* needed him! Instead she died with the painful knowledge her daughter had just been violently raped and left to the mercy of those cruel bastards, and her husband was a coward who'd sat by and allowed it to happen. She knew he could have done more.

The four intruders grabbed the bags of loot as sirens drew closer from outside, sparing Jade any more heinous violation. They took off, leaving Barrett to suffer on the floor, not realising what he was experiencing was a lot more complex than that.

Their paths would cross again.

The Cost Of Vengeance

Jade committed suicide less than a month later, slitting her wrists in the bathtub, plagued by the constant reminder of being raped, and having witnessed the death of her beloved mother.

She held herself responsible for her mum's death, as she'd died trying to protect her, but also blamed her father for not coming to the rescue. She'd always seen him as a heroic figure -- *more than just her dorky dad* -- but in their hour of need, he didn't step up.

Maybe it was an unfair accusation, but she'd seen the same thing her mum had. She'd seen him watching from the floor; he hadn't even tried to stand up and help. Unlike her mother, who died protecting her. Saving her. But there was nothing left to save.

She didn't want to carry on afterwards. Jade had wanted to die there and then, but had to wait a month for those closest to her to unknowingly give her the space to commit the act. She'd left both her grandparents and her dad a note. She apologised to the former for the death of their daughter, and any hurt taking her own life would cause. The latter, she told she could never forgive. She knew deep down he could have helped. He held back, Jade was one-hundred-percent sure of it. She didn't know the reasons why, but her dad could have done more. He could have saved her mum. Saved her.

Why didn't he help!? In Jade's eyes, he was as much to blame for her mother's death as the intruders. As her. As the whole fucking world. A world which she no longer wanted to be a part of.

*

Barrett walked around like a zombie for the months following the brutal death of his wife, and his daughter's suicide. He sold the house, folded the business, and moved out of the city, leaving without a word to any of the friends and family he'd built up over the last fifteen years of his life.

Everyone knew he was hurting and wanted to help, but never knew what to say. *What could you say?* Others, like Alice's parents, blamed Barrett for the death of their daughter and granddaughter, as Jade had revealed some details of the night in her suicide note.

That was the perfect reason for Barrett to flee in the middle of the night and not come back... *until the time was right.* He'd allow everyone to think it was shame, guilt! But the reality of it was he needed time to soak in all the hate, sorrow, and loss. He needed time to prepare for his vengeance.

He truly loved Alice and Jade. They had been his world for the last fifteen years. The light of his life. He woke up every day happy beyond all belief, and watching Jade grow into the beautiful young woman she was becoming was a joy like no other.

But they had to die. The second the intruders cracked him in the head with the bat, everything felt real again. The world he'd been living in wasn't the one he truly wanted, or deserved. The happiness he felt didn't belong to him. It wasn't meant for him. He craved a different kind of pleasure, the joy which could only be derived from vengeance. And in order to get his fill, someone had to wrong him.

The last time Barrett tried manipulating vengeance for himself, he was put in a coma and bargained for his life. If it was meant to be, it was meant to be, just like the incidents before. That was a realisation Barrett came to many years ago.

So he'd waited. He'd waited for a gang of twenty-somethings to jump him, or for him to save someone and pay the consequences. He'd wondered whether it would be a bully in the workplace, or maybe something completely different like road rage. He'd waited and waited; tried to fill the void with distractions which offered a level of pain, but never came close to the experience he needed. He needed legitimate hurt, not manufactured.

In the meantime he'd fallen in love with a beautiful woman and started a family. He'd built a life for himself outside of vengeance. Become a decent member of society. He went to plays, and picked his kid up from school. He did the dishes and cooked dinner. He paid bills and brought polish, had discussions about what vacuum cleaner to purchase. He saved up points at the petrol station for money off coupons.

He hadn't become something he hated, just something he was never meant to be.

But the home invasion *was* meant to be.

It was a sign the whole vengeance process Barrett had almost perfected wasn't done with him yet. Not only that, but there were new levels to hit.

He'd survived plenty of physical pain down the years in order to take his retribution, but what about emotional? And not the emotion of recovering from his injuries, but something much much bigger. The pain and emotion of true love, of unbelievable loss you couldn't recover from. To losing a wife he truly loved with every fibre of his being to a random act of extreme violence. To his daughter dying with nothing but pain and hurt in her broken torn-out heart. To losing a life which he'd built for himself and had ushered in an era of peace and calm.

It was a whole new world of vengeance for Barrett to explore, and revel in.

First, he needed to let the loss infect his soul, which was an easier task than normal. Barrett thought about Alice and Jade every single day. He missed them more than even his parents. They were his everything, and the idea of life without them tortured him. It gave him endless nightmares and unrivalled depression. He'd wake up thinking Alice was asleep beside him, or worry how Jade's day was going. He constantly allowed himself to believe they were alive, and then feel the crushing loss over and over at the realisation he'd never see them again. He'd lost them with his inaction. He was to blame.

He let other thoughts in, too. He'd jumble the images of their wedding day together with the knife penetrating Alice's belly and the look of disappointment in her eyes as she died knowing her husband hadn't helped her. He thought about the autopsy afterwards, revealing Alice had been pregnant, and how he'd lost more children that day than he thought.

He'd think about all the times he'd made Jade giggle as a baby, and laugh as a little cute toddler, then he'd stitch them together with the image of the intruder ploughing his daughter with his bent cock on the floor of their family home. The blood pouring from her ruined cunt as the asshole took her innocence.

He'd let the tears freely flow down his face as he remembered discovering his baby girl in the bathroom with her wrists slit and the note she left blaming him for both their deaths. He'd consume the guilt and agree with her; let it fuel his rage until he was ready to destroy everything within reach.

Man he felt alive.

Such hatred and undiluted anger. Such hurt and authentic pain. He was fuelled with violence straight from the fiery depths of hell as he readied himself to take the ultimate vengeance.

Barrett had always wondered whether there was more to feel, even after he'd stopped searching. He wasn't sure if he could push things any further than what he'd done to those fucking wannabe rapists after waiting six years for them. The release he'd felt taking his vengeance on them that night was beyond description. The bliss he felt walking home in the storm afterwards, letting the rain wash away his sins - but letting him keep the memories forever was a reward.

It had felt like peak vengeance. Six years he'd waited! Six years! Such a long time for something which was over in a night, but lasted a life-time in his mind. It may not have fulfilled him forever, but it never failed to bring a smile to his face.

But now he understood there was more to be had. The suffering and vengeance of loss was something he'd never considered before. Loss to him had been the doctors worried he'd never walk again, or his brain would never function quite right after the latest beating. It almost seemed silly now. The loss of those he loved was a far superior pain, one which excited Barrett. He'd been missing out. But no longer.

Barrett's love and loss of his wife and daughter would take his vengeance to extremes he never knew. To heights not previously thought possible. He would fucking annihilate each and every one of them, and the afterglow would be heavenly. A spiritual experience.

Try as he might, he couldn't fully comprehend the feeling which awaited him, how powerful it would be. But he knew he'd find out one day. It was his destiny. His addiction to vengeance would lead him to this new nirvana.

But he needed to suffer beforehand. He had to carry on thinking about his loving wife and beautiful daughter, and how they were taken down before their time. How they were defiled and killed in front of him. How his unborn child was stabbed before he even knew of its existence.

He needed to think about the life his daughter could have had, what she would have become. He imagined how pleased he'd be with her finishing school. Going to college and university. Walking her down the aisle and looking around her first house. He pictured the grandkids which could now never be. He hadn't just lost the life of his wife and daughter, but subsequently a whole generation. An extended family.

He needed to obsess over every little detail of lost, destruction, blame, and guilt.

They'd left him alive to suffer, so he *would* suffer like no man had ever suffered before. He deserved to suffer, he knew that. He could have saved them, and helped them recover from the ordeal afterwards. Instead, he had watched so he could feel all the hate and pain he felt now. Barrett deserved to suffer, then he deserved his vengeance.

*

Barrett drifted for the next year. His once polite demeanour and well dressed presentation were replaced with endless nightmares and sleeping rough as he found himself homeless. He'd received more than the odd kick as the took to living on the streets. Was spat on and sworn at more times than the rest of his life combined, but he never retaliated. Never caused a scene, or stood up for himself. He didn't need those kind of distractions. He had a higher purpose, a greater goal.

The new lifestyle suited him. Outside, living under the harsh elements, felt right for his mindset. *A winter of discontent.* Rain and frost pushed him to his already fragile limits. He could take a punch, but could he survive a cold winter outside with nothing but a threadbare jacket? He had money. The sale of his home, and the payout of his wife's life insurance, meant he was set for life, but he didn't need those comforts. He needed to be punished. He needed to feel the pain and lost inside him in every moment. Living in shop doorways and under filthy tunnels gave him all the time in the world to stew.

The baseball bat to the head during the attack brought back

the headaches he'd taken years to recover from too. They were never fully gone, but had become more just a hum in the background. Now they were back, and almost crippling at times. He considered telling a doctor about them, but didn't. He liked the constant reminder. A link to his past.

Plus, it was yet another way to punish himself. Another thing to eat at his soul.

In his weaker moments, Barrett sometimes wondered what would've happened if he had put a stop to the attack. If he'd grabbed the gun and shot those motherfuckers right there and then. If he stood up and protected his wife and daughter in their moment of need.

He would hopefully still be living with them, working through the ordeal as a family. His wife would try to be strong, but would be hurting inside, while he knew his daughter would have fallen to pieces. He remembered thinking at the time they could have stood side-by-side to get their vengeance, but that was just a pipe-dream. It wasn't Jade. She was a sweet kid. A typical teenager, more worried about what the girls at school would think than whose ass she could kick.

And what about the unborn baby?

He believed he'd still be happy, but it was an illusion. The more time he spent thinking about it, the more he understood it was never to be. It wouldn't have lasted. What happened was the inevitable conclusion in order for him to enter the next stage of his life.

All those years ago in The Coffee Home, he'd pondered what the next level of vengeance would be. How he could push it further? What more could he suffer? Deal out? Having his wife and child raped and murdered was the answer. The start of a new story of vengeance.

It had taken fifteen years to manifest, but would be worth the wait. Without the time put in to create the stakes, there'd be nothing to lose. He thought a year or six had been playing the long game, but this was some next level commitment. It had happened unknowingly, but with the power of hindsight it had always been building towards this.

His wife and daughter were in his life to be a sacrifice. For him to experience a loss greater than his own. They had both played a pivotal part in his existence without truly understanding how. The love of a tender woman and caring child was one thing; the loss of them under such barbaric circumstances was something all together more.

They'd played their part in this game, and now he had to play his. He'd let the suffering simmer long enough. His fall from grace had been mighty. He'd built himself a life so he would have something to lose, then he'd set it all on fire with one inaction, and began the grieving process.

From the moment he didn't fight back, everything had been set in motion for the time he came to get his vengeance... and now was the fucking time. He needed to remove himself from the shadows and take the action his wife had wanted from him on the faithful night.

It may have been too late for her and Jade, but it was never about them. None of this was. His daughter's life was one long sacrifice. She had lived and died so he could get his vengeance.

Looking For Vengeance

Barrett always had a knack for tracking down the fuckers who attacked him. *My vengeance won't be denied.*

Scotty Turner hadn't been difficult; the bullying dickhead sat a few rows over from him in class whenever he wasn't suspended.

The drunk teens had been a different matter. Barrett got a half decent look at them - despite what he told the police - but the city still housed hundreds-of-thousands of people, and tracking down four delinquents was no easy task. By the time he was released from hospital and recovered enough to venture outside, there was no point checking the crime scene. Any evidence of the attack was long gone, plus the police had already taken that route.

Instead, Barrett had to go on what he already knew. He remembered the brand of beer they threw at him, checked the local off-licence's in the area, asked the different shop keepers; retold what the thugs looked like, and eventually got a lead which led him to their gang.

Under different circumstances, Barrett could have become a detective, but police brutality was frowned upon, and Barrett wasn't going to let these assholes off with a warning.

For the two savage fucks who'd put Barrett in a coma, he discreetly followed their family and friends. The pair's names and reputation were public knowledge after the assault had made local news, so it was easier to know where to start, even after they'd skipped town. It became all about patience, something Barrett had in abundances. In the end it was the woman who Barrett initially flirted with who unknowingly gave him their location. He didn't waste any time tracking them down once he knew.

In spite of the long wait as they served six years in prison, the aspiring rapists weren't difficult to catch up with. Barrett got word of their pending release and simply followed them from the gates. He stalked the newly freed trio back to the abandoned building and returned later in the night with a crowbar in hand, and murderous revenge on his mind.

They should have used the few hours before his return to get the fuck out of dodge, but instead snorted coke, downed some bevvies, and ended up pulpy unrecognisable messes on an already stained floor. *Probably an anti-drugs infomercial there.*

Despite their hasty exit from his home, the gang who raped and murdered his wife and kid left very little evidence behind. They'd all worn gloves, and took their weapons with them, leaving no potential pre-gloved finger prints. Alice had scratched and clawed at two of them -- *and she and Jade both had plenty of their bodily fluids inside them* -- but no matches were found. Maybe the police could have identified one of them via the tattoo, but that was Barrett's lead, not theirs. He told the cops the same story he told everyone else: they wore masks and knocked him out; he saw very little.

If he told them everything he knew, they could have narrowed the search down, and maybe found the group, but Barrett wasn't about to wait twenty-five years for them to be released from prison. He was getting on now, and had already waited far too long between different retributions. He didn't doubt a twenty-five-year wait would crank up the thirst and eventual bliss to an absolutely divine level, but why chance it? He'd waited long enough for another go on the vengeance ride, and *his* sacrifice was already sufficient to get the desired experience.

No, he was going to be the one to find them and make them fucking suffer. He was going to deliver swift, violent, merciless justice. Time behind bars wasn't what these fucking depraved pigs needed for the heinous acts they'd committed; these cunts needed putting the fuck down. Good old-fashioned vigilante justice, and Barrett was just the person to deliver it.

He'd even gotten himself a brand new - albeit old and rusty - crowbar, just for the occasion. He named it Jade.

Fuck the police, this was Barrett's payback. This was his vengeance!

*

Sixteen months passed before Barrett returned to the scene of the crime. He'd spent the vast majority of it living on the streets, and decided to continue the lifestyle during his search for the murdering bastards. He only briefly considered using his savings to put himself up in a hotel, get a fresh shower, and scrub away the year of dirt ingrained in his skin. He thought about maybe getting a haircut and hiding away the few greys which were starting to peek through his dirty matted hair. A decent meal or two wouldn't hurt either. But, ultimately he'd grown accustomed to living in poverty, it was now a part of who he was.

For ninety-nine-percent, it wasn't a lifestyle, it wasn't a choice; it was a living fucking hell. But, for Barrett, it had its advantages. Not only had living this way given him time to go mad with grief and hate, it had also turned him invisible. No one saw the homeless, at least not in the way they saw other people. IIe could sit and watch the world go by just like he used to in the coffeeshop, but with even less attention and interaction. It was a disguise.

It also led to him looking a lot different. He'd lost weight, and his face was gaunt. His previously full hair was thinning, and the layer of grime had changed his complexion. He was unrecognisable from the married father and business owner of two years ago. The look blended well with his broken nose and scars, far more than meetings and deadlines ever had. He was still tall and strong, but it was even more hidden beneath his rough exterior and ragged clothes. He liked the 'nothing to lose' symbolism of being homeless too.

Together, it all felt very right to Barrett. *Karma and vengeance combined.*

He tested his new power of invisibility by staking a spot near the local corner-shop Alice's parents frequented. Three days after hanging around the area -- *and being shooed away by the shopkeeper multiple times* -- Alice's parents walked right past him. Neither gave him a second glance, despite being less than a couple of feet away. They'd have definitely wanted a word or two, but he was invisible to them, just as suspected.

It did give Barrett an opportunity, however, to survey the in-laws who'd always treated him well, despite having their doubts. He guessed they'd been proven right in the end, but it was no consolation to anyone.

Both had aged ten years in the sixteen months since their daughter's and granddaughter's deaths. They looked on the verge of kicking it themselves. Neither had adapted to life after losing a child; how could they? Barrett could empathise; he too looked completely different after thinking about Jade's death every single day. He examined the sadness permanently etched on their withering faces, the loss of life in their eyes. Both were waiting to die. They had each other, but they were no longer complete. A life's work ruined.

He'd get vengeance for them. They deserved their daughter's killer to be torn apart, even if they were in no state to do it themselves. He quietly promised them he'd get in some extra shots just for them. He'd prolong the agony the murdering rapist would go through on their behalf. He'd let the fucker know, too. *This one's from mum and dad.* he'd say as he caved in the cunt's skull with his crowbar. It was fitting; the husband and memory of the granddaughter would combine to take revenge. Barrett smiled at the thought as the old couple disappeared into the shop and out of his life forever.

The city had changed in his absence. It had been their home for the last fifteen years, but had to move on without them; it didn't stop the memories flooding back. His former home now belonged to a new young family, though the exterior still looked the same. It hadn't fallen into disrepair and become one of those murder houses; it carried with it the same purpose it had before Alice's and Jade's deaths. The streets he once walked were the same streets, but half the shops were either different, or now closed. The weather was still shit, so that had stayed the same at least, despite the seasons passing. The people looked like the same people he saw every day in his previous life, but he had no real way of knowing how many had come and gone.

It didn't matter, there were only four people he was interested in identifying: the murdering scum who killed his family. He hoped and prayed they'd stayed in the city and hadn't become part of the change.

*

Barrett remembered the gruff aggressive voice of the leader. The one with the bent dick who took his daughter's virginity and stabbed his wife multiple times with the knife Barrett used to use to carve the meat for their Sunday roasts. He recalled the annoying disgusting snort one of the bat carriers had. He'd replayed the snort in his mind constantly since then. Knew the exact tone. Could replicate it. Most importantly, could identify it. He'd also thought about the stupid fucking jig the asshole who whacked his wife with the bat did after he'd hit her.

It wasn't much to go on, and Barrett certainly couldn't ask

around about a gruff voice, disgusting snort, and stupid fucking dance, but it was a way to separate them in his mind. The gruff voice, the terrible snort, and the ridiculous dance, he'd take vengeance on all of them.

Which left the thug with the skull rose tattoo. The one who'd raped Alice. Barrett decided the tattoo was his best lead. He remembered thinking at the time the tattoo had a certain uniqueness to it; a skull with rose eyes. As the asshole brutally defiled Alice, more of the tattoo had begun to show. Barrett had seen petals and vines wrapped around the base of the skull as he got a full look at the art. Initials too: R.T etched on the skull's forehead.

Barrett didn't give a fuck what the letters meant, but it probably made the tattoo one of a kind. He could work with that.

He hoped the tattoo had been inked within the city. The piece looked good, so no doubt a picture of it would be on display in the parlour where it was created. Whether that could help him or not, he wasn't sure, but it was a place to start. He began to search every tattoo parlour he could find within the city limits.

It turned out, like everyone else, tattoo artists didn't like having bums in their establishments. *Invisible to everyone but shopkeepers.* He spent long enough in each shop to get a look at the immediate displays and some sample books before he was thrown out, though. While there were plenty of skulls and roses, none came close to matching the design he was looking for.

Why the city needed so many tattoo parlours was beyond him. The search felt endless. Every time he crossed one off, another would spring up. And that was just here. If the rapist piece of shit had it done elsewhere, which was a distinct possibility, the search could take a lifetime.

He occasionally tried asking one of the artists about who

could have inked such a design, hoping it would trigger some inspiration or memory, but everything felt like a highly guarded secret -- *or they don't want to send business elsewhere.* Barrett couldn't exactly tell them it was to help him track down his family's rapist murderers so he could rip them apart and send them to hell in tiny pieces, although on the more frustrating of days, he was tempted.

At night, he'd retreat to the home he'd made for himself at the back of an empty shop and cry at the thought of never catching up with the cunts who'd taken his life from him. He didn't believe for a second he wouldn't find them; he knew he would. But he'd force himself to believe otherwise. Create more pain and suffering. Torture his shattered soul further, so when the time came to exact his vengeance, it would be even juicier.

He knew all the tricks of the trade after seeking retribution multiple times down the years. This was going to be the ultimate experience. His masterpiece. He fully intended to squeeze every drop of joy he could from it, and in order to achieve that, he needed to put himself through maximum misery.

*

The search had gone on fruitlessly for five months before Barrett caught a lucky break.

As he sat on a toilet in a vandalised bathroom, popping the blisters which had accumulated on his filthy feet, he heard a nasally disgusting snort come from the stall next to him.

If you want to find scum, search for it in a scummy place. Five months of hiking up every high street in the city looking for the cunts, and one came along the moment he took a rest. He'd learnt over the years that the world was full of cruel and unusual ironies; he wasn't about to question it when one worked in his favour.

Barrett had never seen any of their faces so had no way of truly identifying the guy on sight, but no one else on the planet had that fucked up snort.

This was the guy. Every fibre in his body told him so. He forced his crumbling shoes back on and made his way to the grubby sinks opposite the stalls. He twisted the loose tap, which spluttered and dribbled ice cold water into the basin. Barrett used his soiled jacket sleeve to wipe away a layer of dirt and grime from the cracked mirror in front of him to give himself a reflection of the Snorter's stall while he washed his hands.

The door swung open to some six foot rhino-looking motherfucker, which only reaffirmed Barrett's belief: this was his man. Right height, build, and fucking snort. Unless those snorts came pre-packaged with guys this size, Barrett had stuck gold.

The Snorter took his place alongside Barrett at the sinks and started washing his hands, while hacking up a ball of phlegm and spitting it onto the sordid floor. He could have just as easily spat the wad into the sink and washed it down the drain, but clearly the guy was a fucking asshole. Barrett smirked to himself. This was one-hundred-percent one of the men he was looking for.

He'd prepared for this moment plenty, thought about it every night for nearly two years, but the circumstances in which it happened caught him off guard. He'd expected to spy them from a distance, maybe stake out an address or drug den after some fortuitous tip. The last thing he imagined was to be standing side-by-side with one of the assholes in the gents.

His mind briefly went back to the last time he took vengeance. That too had begun in a bathroom; he'd already hacked the guy's arm off by this point. *Circle of life?* He didn't have the time to do that right now, despite having the crowbar stashed in his jacket, so he tried a different approach instead.

"Come here often?" he asked, putting on a slight accent in case his voice was as recognisable as some of their attributes.

He doubted they'd remembered much about him, though. They'd probably imprinted the vision of his wife's and daughter's cunts in their heads, but wouldn't remember a single thing about the useless pathetic father beaten on the floor. *That's about to change.*

"You some kind of hobo fag?" the brute replied, with another trademark foul snort as he twisted the tap off.

"Just making conversation," Barrett answered defensively, trying to hide the smirk brewing inside him at making first contact with the man he'd soon kill.

"Fucking weirdo," the Snorter said, before turning to leave.

Barrett wanted to smash him over the back of the head right there. Dunk his head in one of the shitty toilets and waterboard the motherfucker until he gave up his friends. But two other rough-looking bastards entered the grimy facilities. Instead, he followed the man, out hoping he'd lead him to the others. It was unlikely, and Barrett knew he'd already used up a lifetime of luck finding this cunt the way he did, but one could hope.

If not, he'd just follow him for a while and then beat the information out of him. Either way, the Snorter wouldn't be seeing a new day.

Vengeance On A Snorter

Rain fittingly pissed from the grey sky as Barrett followed the Snorter through the city streets. He kept a distance behind, but doubted the guy would turn and notice. The Snorter walked like he was the fucking *man*; no-one would touch him. Barrett wondered whether he had a reputation, or if his size exacerbated his confidence. *And he wasn't even the biggest of the four.*

The Snorter stopped for a bite to eat at a greasy spoon, but wasn't joined by anyone, as Barrett stealthily watched him from across the road. The rain continued to pour, and the building he leant against offered little protection, but Barrett wouldn't have it any other way.

This all felt right. It was all finally happening.

He was excited. The search hadn't been getting him down, but he'd been unable to come up with a plan B if it didn't work out. Then it all just fell right into his lap. He hadn't even had the opportunity to take it in yet. One second, his feet are killing him and he's wondering whether he should buy a cream or some insoles ... the next, he's on a full blown manhunt with nothing but pure and barbaric vengeance in mind.

The man across the street enjoyed his mediocre cheeseburger and salty fries, having no fucking clue what was coming to him. Barrett, however, had compiled a laundry list of ghastly ideas over the last two years.

After the asshole finished his grub, he met with some shady motherfucker in a side street to score a bag of something Barrett could only assume was coke. Having never been a drug person himself, his knowledge was limited, but you didn't meet a meth-head-looking tweaker in the pissing rain for a bag of flour. The Snorter had his nose in it before he'd even left the grimy side street. Maybe that was how he'd developed his vile nasal idiosyncrasy.

Barrett kept a watchful eye on him from a distance for the rest of the afternoon, until he ended up in a betting shop. Peering through the doorway, he could see a couple of what he assumed were regulars greet the man as he entered; none of them were the size of the home invaders. Barrett took a place near the shop doorway and sat down for the rest of the evening as the rain continued to splash, forming puddles around him as he collected his thoughts and planned what to do next.

He grabbed hold of the crowbar tucked away inside his jacket like a comfort blanket. It hadn't left his side since he'd found it, but it also hadn't seen any use. The city hadn't treated him kindly since his return, and he could have pulled it out plenty of times, but hadn't. Much like he'd ignored the bullshit during his sabbatical, he had the same rules here. Plenty of assholes deserved a crack across the temple with the weapon, but Jade wasn't meant for them. The sharpened crowbar was meant for the cunt inside the betting shop, and his soon-to-be-dead rapist friends.

The Snorter emerged deep into the night when the betting shop finally closed. A big smile on his face suggested it had been a lucrative evening, enforced by several of the other chummy customers calling him a 'lucky cunt' and sharing in some banter as they all ignored the homeless man sitting at their feet.

I truly am invisible.

The group parted ways as the rain intensified, after having previously eased as day turned to night. Several darted towards their cars - the only ones remaining in a parking lot across the street - while the Snorter set off on foot.

Barrett followed him once again, away from the empty high-street towards a nearby park. It was normally a hangout spot for the local thugs, but was abandoned due to the heavy rain keeping the riff-raff indoors. The weather had kept most people off the street all evening, and now conveniently seemed no different. Barring the customers who left the betting shop alongside the Snorter, Barrett had barely seen another soul in hours.

A crack of thunder interrupted his thoughts as a flash of lightning laid out the path ahead. Barrett saw the Snorter was heading towards a vandalised subway at the opposite end of the vacant park. The rain covered his footsteps as he continued to follow. As they closed in on the barely-lit tunnel, Barrett picked up the pace and ate up the ground between them, deciding it would be the perfect place to strike.

Go time.

It was the first time Barrett had truly hit a man in over fifteen years, but there was no ring rust. No hesitation or doubt. There was no room for error when it came to vengeance, and Barrett wasn't about to offer any.

He rapidly brought the jagged claw end of the crowbar down against the back of the Snorter's calf as he caught up with him. The overly sharpened claw easily pierced through the Snorter's soaked jeans and tore into the muscle, ripping it in half. A sudden shock of pain bolted through the ambushed man as his leg collapsed and he fell to the piss-stained concrete just inside the tunnel entrance.

A river of crimson poured from the ghastly shredded meat. The Snorter howled in agony and confusion, not having the slightest fucking clue what had happened. He sprawled face down on the unforgiving concrete, reaching for the excruciating pain emanating from the back of his leg. As he touched the wound, he felt the ripped hole in his jeans and the soppy, ruined muscle beneath it.

Only two lights worked inside the tunnel, offering very little illumination as they'd been spray painted over. They shed just enough light for the Snorter to see an outline of his attacker.

"You?" was all the bewildered Snorter could muster as he turned and recognised the bum from the public toilet. "What the hell?" he asked through gritted teeth and riving pain.

"So you recognise me?" Barrett queried, somewhat surprised.

"Is this 'cos I didn't suck your dick you fucking homo?"

Barrett could only laugh. *Oh this asshole is going to die so fucking violently.*

"No. It's because you and your friends killed my family."

It only seemed to further confuse the fallen asshole. Blood continued to cascade from the back of his mangled leg as he squinted at Barrett, as if trying to figure out who exactly he was.

How many times have they pulled this shit not to know right away? Barrett thought, while he waited for the penny to drop.

"I ain't ever killed no one you cunt," Snorter roared, propping himself up. "You got the wrong man."

Barrett smashed the crowbar against his elbow sending a horrible vibration through his body and bruising the bone as the impact dropped him back to the concrete. Then he jammed the crowbar into the exposed calf muscle and wrenched the tear wider, to a chorus of ear piercing shrieks which went unheard by anyone else as they echoed through the grotty tunnel.

"I've got the right man," Barrett informed him as he gripped the blood-soaked crowbar, staring down at the bone he'd unveiled. It felt so fucking good to hurt again. "Nearly two years ago, you and your buddies jumped me in my home. You raped my wife before stabbing her to death. You raped my fourteen-year-old daughter too."

He let his words sit for a moment as tears welled in the corners of his eyes. He considered wiping them away but let them gather. It was only right he also hurt in this moment.

"She committed suicide afterward," he added. The evil in his cracking voice suggested the Snorter and his buddies had all ensured their place in hell... "That's not something a man forgets."

The Snorter fought his agony long enough to twist to his side, trying to get a look at Barrett. While his appearance may have changed drastically he saw a flicker of recognition enter the man's mind.

"I..."

Barrett didn't let him speak, jabbing the crowbar into his ample gut, scraping and drawing blood, but not opening it up to the level he had the calf.

Just 'mild' pain, for his own amusement. A higher dosage would soon follow.

"Tell me where to find the others," Barrett demanded, because it most certainly wasn't a polite request.

"You got the wrong guy, you prick!" His trembling voice betrayed his tough act. Then he snorted in his usual foul manner, which couldn't have contradicted his statement more if he tried. *May as well hold a big fucking sign.*

"Where are they?" Barrett questioned.

"Fuck you!" Snorter responded, trying bravely to get to his feet despite the injured leg.

But Barrett didn't give him a chance, whacking him across the side of the head, partially catching his right ear with the crowbar's claw. The ear wasn't ripped clean off, but it was left hanging by threads of gristle.

Barrett remembered the feeling well, recalling a bottle doing the same to his own ear all those years ago. A lifetime ago now, although he still had the scar.

Snorter wallowed and wailed, unable to decide which part of his ruined body to hold onto in an attempt to alleviate some of the mounting pain.

As he did so, Barrett relieved him of his wallet. Opening it revealed a prize much more valuable than his winnings from the betting shop; his driving license, with name -- Eric Robertson -- and address. Better yet, there was a photo of three little girls, presumably his daughters.

Barrett grinned. A different approach was required.

"I'll make this nice and simple, *Eric*," he said coldly, putting an emphasis on his name. "You give up your three friends, or..." He held up the picture. "I'll take this crowbar, and use it to rape these three innocent angels instead. Eye for an eye, and all that."

"You fucking..."

The crowbar smashed into the other side of Eric's face, loosening his jaw before he finished whatever the fuck he was going to say. It didn't matter to Barrett; the only words he wanted to hear were the whereabouts of his three accomplices. Otherwise, three others would suffer instead.

"That's my final offer," Barrett concluded, like it was a fair trade.

"I didn't rape no-one," Eric put forth in mumbled defence, holding onto his jaw. The injuries were accumulating, and the blood lost was becoming evident . He was going into shock as his stuttered his next words. "You... got... the... wrong... man."

"Have it your way." Barrett pocketed the photo with a suggestive evil smirk on his face, then raised the bloody crowbar high, like a medieval-executioner ready to deliver the killer blow. If Eric wasn't going to give up his mates, then his time was done, and so was his daughters'.

"No... Wait." The Snorter raised his arms, a defeated look on his face. He took a couple of deep breaths, trying to steady his breathing and keep the shock under control. "Look, it wasn't me.. I wasn't the one who murdered your wife... I didn't touch your kid... You can't do this."

"Then tell me where to find the ones who did."

"I've never done anything like that before," he whined in a resigned voice. "I thought we were just robbing the place, then you walked in on us." He had tears in his eyes, but they were caused by his own suffering, not regret.

"You already told me that part," Barrett said. "Although you may have added a 'dumb fuck' at the time."

"Please. Don't hurt my kids."

"I asked the same of you."

"It wasn't me! Did I touch your fucking kid?" Eric yelled.

Barrett smashed the crowbar across his face again, then dug the sharp claw of the crowbar into Eric's nostrils and jerked back, destroying the bone and cartilage as he tore the nose from his face, creating a bloody crater. He then finished the job on the hanging ear, bringing the claw down to server it from the side of Eric's fucked-up head.

Collecting the freed facial features, he tossed them onto Eric's stomach, then brought the crowbar down on top of them in an attempt to smash them into his ribs. The results winded Eric and sent the loose ear and nose tumbling onto the bloody ground.

Eric's screams were deafening as they echoed down the empty tunnel, but still no-one was around to hear. There was no rescue on its way. No one phoning the police to report screams coming from the subway. He was fucked.

"I'm done with this," Barrett said, leveling the crowbar at Snorter's face. "You want to talk about fucking kids, that's what I'm going do right now."

His eyes were ablaze, thoughts of his little girl being raped in front of him as fresh in his mind as the day it happened. And the image of this piece of shit, smashing his head in with a bat while his wife was getting fucked by some tattooed scumbag asshole, was crystal clear.

It was all there for Barrett to see, hear ... hell, he could fucking *smell* the memory. And Eric was one of the ones responsible. His punishment had only just begun.

"Hopefully, when I jam this up the littlest one's innocent cunt," he said, twisting the crowbar in front of Eric's eyes, "it will still have some of Daddy's nose on it. You can smell her unripe pussy."

"Please..." Eric begged, as he struggled to breathe. The nasally snort didn't follow for once, due to the lack of a fucking nose. "Please... Please."

Barrett held the crowbar aloft, ready for the final blow. He held the position long enough to let the former Snorter know the fate of his daughters was up to him. *Loyalty would only get you so far.*

"I haven't seen Tex and Rick for a while, but I know where you can find Jessy," Eric blurted.

"Is he the one who dances like a prick?" Barrett questioned.

Eric couldn't help but smirk. Despite being on the verge of death, and the man causing it threatening to rape his kids, that was exactly who Jessy was. "Yeah. The one who dances like a prick," he reaffirmed.

"Where is he? And remember, I'm keeping hold of the picture and your driving licence, so don't even fucking think about lying to me."

"He'll be at his girl's place. They're inseparable now. Practically live together. She's got him under her thumb. Do anything for her," Eric spilled, like he was conversing with a bud down the pub. "She lives down on Hollow Street, the place with the red door."

Eric's breathing became laboured. His skin had gone so white he was practically translucent. The only colour was the red spilling from the holes in his face and mangled calf. He was ready to die. This was his last chance to save his kids.

"You bullshitting me?"

The Snorter shook his head. Barrett studied him for a moment, nodding his approval at the soon-to-be-dead man telling him the truth.

"You'll leave my daughters alone?" Eric asked, wanting to be at peace before he took his finally breath.

Barrett didn't respond.

Instead, he drove the crowbar into Eric's open mouth and yanked it back, taking a few teeth with him. He raised and brought it down repeatedly, like he was chopping wood, as he crushed and cracked Eric's skull. He tucked the claw end into Eric's armpits and began to wrench at the muscles, having learnt from previous vengeance you could remove a man's arm like that.

Eric's retarded, gurgled screams began to fade in swallowed blood as the brain damage and destruction took its toll. Barrett changed position and ripped Eric's Achilles tendon, before dragging the nearly-dead weight to his feet, just to laugh at him collapsing in on himself as the leg folded.

Then he dug out an eyeball and added it to the froth of blood and teeth in the Snorter's mouth as he choked his final rancid breaths.

But Barrett still wasn't done. Not for what this fuck had done to him and his family. He owed him plenty more pain, even if his heart had stopped beating. He needed to get in a few shots for Alice's parents too.

He beat on the dead body for another hour. Ripped open every muscle and tendon he could find. He'd have ground the bones to dust if he had the means. Two years of pent up anger was unleashed, and Barrett couldn't put a stop to it.

Nor did he want to. And this was just the first of the four.

Dancing With Vengeance

Barrett wasn't concerned about Eric's body being found. He didn't have time to ditch it, and there were no obvious spots to hide the remains, so he left the mess smearing the piss-stained subway floor.

It didn't look recognisable as human, let alone the man formerly known as Eric. Plus, Barrett had taken his driving licence; they wouldn't be identifying him anytime soon. He was certain it would initially be reported as a wild animal attack, though there weren't any wild animals in the city which could have done that.

Himself being the exception.

He headed to Hollow Street, and sure enough one of the houses had a bright red door. Barrett hadn't given much thought to what he would have done if it didn't. Despite his threats, he never intended to harm Eric's innocent little girls. It wasn't his style. At this point, it wouldn't have helped anyway, unless they called the dancing prick Uncle Jessy and knew his exact whereabouts. Which Barrett doubted they did. *Sure can't go back to Eric for answers, either.*

It was early hours of the morning and the rain was still drizzling, but Hollow Street was a hive of activity. Plenty of lights were on inside the tall narrow homes packed into the street, while an abundance of sketchy fuckers were gathered outside the pub at the end of the road, each with a pint in one hand, and a cigarette in the other, unperturbed by the rain as they smoked and loudly conversed.

A couple were fucking in the alley beside the pub, while a guy took a leak on the other side. A fight broke out by the entrance, two beefy guys arguing over a spilt drink. Barrett watched the scuffle, remembering his own altercation in such a place as both men started throwing meaty fists. A few of the smokers quickly broke the fight up, and they all seemed to be laughing and joking about it moments later.

A pair of stray cats fought for scraps closer to Barrett, while a couple of dogs barked at the noise. Music blared from one of the homes near the middle of the street. It was loud enough to cause a major disturbance in any other street at this hour, but not this one. The music house's curtains were drawn back and the lights were on. Barrett could see the home jammed full of people all having a great time, and had no doubts they were fucked up on plenty more than just alcohol.

The music house was three doors up from 'Jessy's girl' - according to the recently deceased Eric. The lights were off in the red door home and Barrett wondered whether they were at the party. It seemed plausible. No way were they sleeping through the racket. The other option was the pub at the end of the street.

Of course they could have been anywhere, including tucked up in bed, but after his chance encounter with the Snorter, Barrett was feeling like this was his night. Jessy was out there ready to fucking die. *The night isn't over yet, not by a long shot.*

Barrett lowered himself to the pavement across from the red door. His knees groaned as he sat -- *it's not the years, it's the mileage.* His filthy, worn jacket was sullied with the Snorter's blood; while the crowbar was safety tucked inside. Anyone walking by would have done a double-take at the obvious red, but no one was looking in his direction. He knew from experience he'd get a few comments if the assholes from the pub walked past, but to anyone not wanting to mock him, he wasn't there.

Invisible, and alone. Free to watch the red door, and plan his next savage vengeance.

He closed his eyes, drowning out the shitty music blasting

from the rowdy house across the street, and instead listened to a mental replay of the Snorter's screams and pleas. The howls of cruel and unusual torture as the steel dug through exposed muscle and tore apart his panicked face. The sweet sound of vengeance, *oh how he had missed it.*

He hadn't harmed another human being in close to sixteen years he calculated. Maybe longer. *Where had the years gone?*

That's right, they'd been preparing him for this precise moment. The blissful feeling surging through his excited body was like no other. The knowledge he'd begun his payback for the death of his wife and kid was hedonistic. He'd taken justice for them ... well, a quarter of it, so far.

The image of Jade being violated in their family home was replaced by the Snorter's mangled, unrecognisable corpse. Her screams and trauma were replaced by his. Sure, he could say he didn't touch her, but he'd been there. *They were all responsible for her death!* Every single one of them would go through the pain she did, and then some.

They had all been dead men walking from the moment they struck Barrett. From the moment they'd assaulted his wife and broken his daughter. Their lives had been extended only because *he* allowed it. They'd been given these extra years due to Barrett's patience and his thirst for pure undiluted vengeance, as he let the misery fully infect his rotted heart.

'Vengeance from loss,' *damn it did feel sweeter.*

He wanted to lie back in orgasmic bliss, but he was only a quarter done. He was only feeling a small portion of what joy there was to absorb. A sample of the pleasure he'd take from ripping these scumbag assholes apart. One fourth of the spiritual awakening this vengeance of all vengeance would ignite within him. Killing these cunts was like rocket-fuel for his tortured and damned soul.

And if killing *one* of those fuckers felt this good...

...His thoughts were interrupted as a voice across the street broke his concentration.

While the voice didn't use the exact words 'that will learn you,' that's what Barrett heard. They were the only words he knew from the dancing cunt, and the sound of his voice for the first time in two years brought the callous remark back.

He saw the prick smash his wife over the head from behind with the bat all over again. Replayed him helping the tattooed asshole strip her bare. He remembered the look of anticipation after the jig, like he was going to get some too. In his mind, the shit-bag was licking his lips and drooling as the tattooed beast tried to snap Alice in half with each brutal thrust.

It all came rushing back at the sound of his voice. The actual words he'd said didn't matter, what mattered was... Barrett had found him.

He opened his eyes and saw a man who matched the size of the baseball bat attacker, opening the red door alongside a woman. Barrett was hoping he'd do the stupid fucking jig for confirmation as he turned the key, but apparently he didn't do it every second of the day.

Fuck it, it has to be him.

He couldn't get a good look at the woman with him, but he saw her arms wrapped around the man's ass. Both were clearly inebriated, and horny as hell. Set to have an all night fuck session to the soundtrack of the loud obnoxious music still spilling out into the night.   Barrett had other plans.

He gave it twenty minutes before crossing the street and jamming the crowbar into the bright red door, breaking into the house with minimum fuss. The booming music covered any noise and no-one was looking in this direction.

No sooner had he crossed the threshold than he could hear the pair banging each other's brains out at the top of the stairs. A pile of discarded clothes led up to them like some kind of deviant breadcrumbs.

The place was a fucking shit hole. The pile of clothes on the stairs could have just as easily been there before Barrett entered, but he'd seen them wearing the same outfits outside. A bunch of dirty sneakers and shoes were spewed over the floor by the front door. Discarded takeaway boxes and cigarette butts littered the mangy carpet. Empty liquor bottles were lined up against the wall, awaiting a recycling day which would never come.

A quick glance down the hall showed Barrett both the living room and kitchen. For such a small space, they had a hell of a lot of junk. *Hoarders.* All kinds of magazines and knick-knacks were dotted around the confined living room. The threadbare sofa looked mouldy as it acted as a replacement clotheshorse.

Piles of what had to be stolen goods waiting to be sold were stacked in the corner of the unkempt room. They weren't subtle about it. One knock on the door from the cops and they'd instantly see the mountain of game consoles and TV's standing suspiciously in the room, but Barrett presumed the cops didn't venture this way often. They'd probably have to arrest the whole fucking street, judging from what he'd seen so far.

The kitchen sink was overflowing with a mish-mash of plates and cups in filthy stale water, while half-eaten food was left rotting away on the sides. Barrett was sure if he opened the fridge door the smell wouldn't leave him for the rest of his life. The house already had an extremely pungent funk in the air. *Stale piss, whiskey, and cigarettes.*

He didn't remember Jessy smelling during the home invasion, but then he'd been having a bit of a sensory overload at the time. Still, it was the kind of detail he normally picked up on, so he wondered whether this was all the girlfriend's doing, or whether they'd fallen on hard times. The stash of stolen goods in the living room suggested they could be getting by, but the house resembled a fucking crack-den.

He quietly ascended the stairs as the boisterous moans got louder. The girlfriend's room was to the left at the top, with a small bathroom next to it. The couple were facing away from Barrett as Jessy jackhammered his dick into the girl's willing ass while she shouted encouragement, with her head against the pillows and her bony backside aimed in the air.

"Fuck me harder, babe! Don't be a pussy. Destroy my ass!"

"I'm going to fucking demolish you! You won't be able to walk for a week."

"You promise?" she taunted, with glee in her voice as sweat poured from her greasy hair.

Jessy picked up the pace. His long, hanging balls slapped against her gaunt ass.

"Yes. Yes. Yes." The girl shouted as Jessy went into overdrive, ramming his rod in and out of her gaping asshole like a pneumatic drill.

Barrett watched from the doorway, the enthralled couple both unaware of his intrusion.

That changed in a hurry when Barrett added to the sexcapade by ramming the crowbar up Jessy's asshole. Easily enough, thanks to the aid of plenty of ass sweat, some suspected previous pegging, and good-old-fashion brute force.

He jammed the steel bar in a good few inches deep before ripping Jessy's anus inside out in one swift, excruciating, messy tug. It sent Jessy into a frenzied agony but didn't stop him jizzing inside his girl like he was having the orgasms to end all orgasms, *which he might just be doing.*

Blood and shit oozed from his tattered corn hole and ran down his legs, soaking the yellowed sheets beneath him.

His girlfriend howled, but her shouts were in the thralls of her own sexual ecstasy. She was still completely unaware of

Barrett, or the unholy experience her man had just been put through. She laughed as Jessy fell from her ass to the floor, still screaming; clearly she couldn't tell the difference between the sound of pleasure, and the sound of pain.

Barrett understood; the two in his mind were one and the same. While he had enjoyed them both separately at different points in his life, their relationship to him was as one.

Furthermore, even when getting his asshole ripped out, Jessy had spit his cum all over his girl's backside, *what more proof did you need?*

Barrett considered how naming his crowbar after his dead daughter seemed inappropriate now it had been inside a man's ass, albeit one who deserved it. He looked in awe at the blood and shit-stained mess the liberation of Jessy's anus caused. Chunks of meat and excrement hung from the rusty bar, joining any remaining gunk left from Eric. A trail of crimson and brown marked Jessy's fall from the bed to the grotty floor.

Finally it registered with the woman someone else was in the room. She looked back from her vulnerable position and saw Barrett standing at the end of the bed with the soiled crowbar. Her mouth dropped open in a disbelieving gawk before her eyes tracked Jessy on the floor and narrowed in on the blood and shit covering the lower half of his naked body. His continued howling suddenly made more sense.

Before she could scream for help, Barrett leapt forward and smacked her over the head with the filthy crowbar, with enough force to knock her out, but not enough to kill her. He wasn't here for the girlfriend, but he wouldn't allow her to spoil his vengeance either. He grabbed the woman by the hair and dragged her from the bed, across the blood and shit and out the room as her consciousness waned.

He tossed her into the small, disgusting bathroom and slammed the door shut. *She won't want to see what happens next.*

Barrett manoeuvred the chest of drawers from the bedroom to the front of the bathroom door to trap her inside, and give himself an early warning for any escape attempt. If she knew what was good for her, she'd stay inside the room until he was long gone, and her man was long fucking dead.

Barrett then turned his attention to Jessy. It occurred to him he hadn't checked the guy's name, or really confirmed in any other way he was the man Barrett was looking for, but it was too late now. *Not like I could reconstruct the asshole.*

The sound of his voice had been all the evidence Barrett needed. Even if he'd imagined the words said, he was sure the voice was correct. Plus, his size matched, and Eric had given this as the address. He was *almost* certain this was the correct guy.

Barrett gave *hopefully* Jessy a few more light taps with the crowbar as the injured and embarrassed man slithered on the floor, pathetically trying to protect himself. Now he'd shot his load and lost a couple of pints of blood to a back alley proctectomy, his dick had shrivelled up and gone into hiding.

"What's your name?" Barrett finally asked.

Jessy whimpered on the bedroom floor. His shredded ass felt like an inferno. He was a big man used to getting his way in any confrontation, but hadn't even heard the bell ring. He desperately wanted to show some fight, yet the volcano of blood and shit pouring from the cavernous gap where his butthole once was had rendered him completely fucking useless.

"Jessy," the man reluctantly confirmed, much to Barrett's relief.

Wouldn't that have been embarrassing if it wasn't. Although judging by the stack of stolen goods in the downstairs living room this cunt's guilty of something either way.

Still, Barrett was here for vengeance. For vigilante justice against one of the four men who had raped and murdered his wife and daughter. Not to reprimand some filthy dickhead for petty theft, so he was pleased he had the right guy.

"Where are your friends Tex and Rick at, Jessy?"

"I don't…"

Barrett placed the sharp bar against Jessy's withered dick and balls. The keen point punctured his ball sack with ease as Barrett applied the pressure. Dark blood dribbled from the wound. Jessy wanted to roll over and protect himself from the excruciating pain which had been added to the immense agony he was already suffering, but any movement with the crowbar positioned how it was would make him a eunuch.

"Think carefully before you tell me you don't know who they are," Barrett suggested. He was itching to pulverise this motherfucker, but refrained. He needed the location of the last two.

Then, all bets were off.

"Who are you?"

"I've just been through this with your buddy Eric; I'm not repeating myself."

"Eric? Is he…"

"I wouldn't worry about him. He's the one who gave you up."

"Now you want me to give up Tex and Rick?"

Barrett nodded, secretly hoping the man would make it difficult.

"I ain't no rat." Jessy spat at Barrett, but the phlegmy wad didn't make it to Barrett; it fell short and landed on Jessy's own chest.

"I was hoping you'd say that," Barrett informed him, before he ripped Jessy's balls clean from his body and inserted the crowbar in the new hole, ready to turn him into a puppet on a stick.

Soaked in Vengeance

Jessy had been a tough son-of-a-bitch. *Stubborn and prideful to a fault.* When he said he wasn't a rat, he fucking meant it. Prying off his cock and balls hadn't been enough, nor shoving the crowbar back up his ruptured asshole for sloppy seconds. Jessy knew he was going to die for the sins he'd committed, and accepted it.

Not willingly; he wasn't happy about it, but he wasn't going to beg. And he made it damn clear he wasn't going to talk! He'd take his punishment, and violent death, but wouldn't drag his friends down with him. He'd told Barrett to go fuck himself a number of times. To do his worst, which Barrett duly obliged.

He took everything Barrett could dish out. Quite frankly, Barrett was shocked by the amount of unrelenting medieval punishment Jessy absorbed; he was even a little jealous. He could have gone for a beating like that himself, *maybe minus the dick and ass removal.*

He hadn't thought Jessy the toughest of the group, but clearly he was. The dancing dickhead could take a whipping. More than a whipping; his fucking asshole had been removed. That could have been enough to kill him right there. Barrett figured the job was pretty much done when he was whimpering on the floor, but he sucked it up and only got more resolute after that. *Credit where credit's due.*

Under different circumstances, maybe they could have been friends, trading stories about their unique pain threshold and ability to take a fucking thrashing. But you don't become buddies with the people responsible for your family's deaths. You fucking obliterate them and take your vengeance!

Jessy was undoubtedly a big rugged loyal bastard. He'd been true to his word, and hadn't given his friends up. He wouldn't have, either, no matter what other torture Barrett inflicted, but things changed when Barrett dragged Jessy's semi-conscious naked girlfriend from the dingy bathroom.

It turned out Eric was right about Jessy's infatuation. While the prick didn't want to give up his mates, he couldn't stand by and watch Barrett torture his girlfriend either. Him getting destroyed was one thing, he could take it, but her... Once Barrett worked that out, it was just a matter of time, and the right amount of pain.

Barrett started off easy by giving her a few slaps to wake her up, then made her beg Jessy to give up Tex and Rick as she gawked at her mutilated boyfriend. Barrett promised her she'd be next as her eyes locked in on his detached dick and balls. Her hands wrapped around her tits, knowing exactly what Barrett meant.

He didn't think to ask her if she knew of their whereabouts herself, but was pretty sure if she did she'd have spilt the beans right away. She didn't have Jessy's resilience, and this wasn't her fight.

Jessy kept apologising to Mia - the girlfriend - but refused to apologise to Barrett, even when he worked out who he was. Like Eric, he played the 'I'm not the one who raped your wife and kid card,' although he added he would have, given the chance.

The cunt was asking for it. *Is he enjoying the beating?* Barrett once again wondered, with a flicker of envy.

He soon changed his tune when Barrett's slaps to Mia turned to whacks with the steel crowbar. The welts from the vicious blows instantly sprang up on her naked skinny body as Barrett went to town. He figured there wasn't much more he could take from Jessy, having already claimed his cock, balls, and asshole, but he could rip out his heart, first figuratively, then literally. Eventually, he'd have his fucking pride too.

Mia begged Barrett to stop, but he wasn't the one she needed to bargain with. Only Jessy could put an end to the brutality, Barrett told her as he snapped one of her arms with a vicious blow. The sound of steel on bone sent her into shock at first, before the pain hit. Unlike Jessy, she couldn't take a beating, but it was only going to get worse for her.

Barrett scratched the claw of the bar down one of her legs, leaving a trail of blood, then threatened to gouge out an eye. His own eyes were locked on Jessy the whole time. The girlfriend was just a means to an end. A pawn. He let her roll around on the bed, bleeding and broken, while he planned his next move.

Barrett tied Jessy up, then broke both his legs and dug the crowbar into what remained of them. He briefly gagged the fucker while he was making him a cripple, as the shouts and screams were getting close to rising above the shitty music -- which was somehow still fucking booming.

He gagged Mia too. After she'd begged Jessy to put a stop to all this, there wasn't really anything more for her to say. She didn't have the answers Barrett wanted, and would only make extra noise with all her crying.

Jessy was on the verge of passing out multiple times, but Barrett wouldn't allow it and kept slapping him awake. He wanted Jessy to suffer every second he could for his involvement in the deaths of Alice and Jade, but there was also the more immediate need of finding the other two men responsible.

Word would soon get back to them about Jessy and Eric. The sooner he knew their location, the sooner he could finish his vengeance, while still having the upper hand.

Plus, he wasn't going to let this stubborn bastard win. Barrett's ego needed Jessy to talk, to give in, to be the fucking rat he swore not to be. While he didn't look like a winner with his asshole ripped apart and his cock lying on the floor next to him, not getting the information from Jessy would count as a loss to

Barrett.

Not fucking happening.

Once Jessy was disabled and awake, Barrett dug the sharp end of the crowbar into Mia's shoulder and started trying to yank her arm clean off in front of him. He had initially felt sick, torturing the poor woman after dragging her from the bathroom, but he knew it was for the greater good.

However, by the time her arm was half-hanging from her body, he was starting to enjoy himself. The bloodlust had kicked in. He told Jessy he was going to die no matter what, but whether Mia followed was up to him. With the arm almost off, Jessy finally caved. The big pleading eyes of his distraught, wrecked girlfriend cracked his stubborn defence. Jessy was loyal, but his loyalties changed just before Mia passed out. She was on the verge of dying, but at least she knew her man was going to get her out of this as she fell unconscious.

It's almost sweet.

Jessy told Barrett about the gym Tex and Rick ran a few towns over. They'd moved from the city nearly a year back after a succession of successful big scores, having upgraded from robbing houses. While Eric and Jessy squandered their ill-gained riches on gambling and booze, the other two had put together a nice little nest egg to go legit.

Their days of theft, rape, and murder were behind them, they'd joked on their last night in the city. Clean and healthy living from there on in. "You can only get away with the shit we do for so long," Tex had told Jessy as parting words. From the pile of stolen goods stashed in the living-room Barrett surmised Jessy still thought he could get away with it a little longer. *Not anymore, his time was up.*

There wasn't any more Barrett could get out of Jessy, as the cunt lay mutilated on the bedroom floor with half his blood having exited his body. However, Jessy wanted one last thing from Barrett. No more resistance, or tough guy act. His pride and ego gone. He just had one last dying request before his trip to hell. The same thing Eric had asked, only, swapping out the daughters for his girlfriend Mia. He wanted Barrett to leave her alone now he'd gotten what he needed. He'd won. Just leave her alone, after making sure she got medical attention and would survive.

Barrett declined the request.

After smashing Jessy to jelly with the crowbar, he did the same to Mia. She only briefly regained consciousness, just enough to know it was the end for her, then he stuck the crowbar through her fucking skull.

He hadn't planned on killing Mia when he entered the house, and had wanted to avoid it, but she knew too much. If he left her alive, she might get word to Tex and Rick, or inform the police and have them interfere before he'd finished his vengeance. She was a witness to his brutality, and unfortunately for her, she had to die. Maybe he could have tied her up somewhere, but when he was in that sort of frenzied mood, Barrett had no off switch.

In the aftermath, he sat on the edge of the bed, a blood-soaked mess. He contemplated what he'd done, and where his thirst for vengeance had led him. For the first time, he'd knowingly taken an innocent life. He'd been responsible for the death of other innocent before, when he burnt down the building, but that was collateral damage and he hadn't lost much sleep over it.

However, he'd killed Mia in cold blood; there was no denying it. She was in a relationship with a scumbag rapist murdering asshole, and was obviously involved in some shady shit herself, but still, she didn't deserve what happened to her.

That was on Barrett. His cross to bear.

On his quest for vengeance, he'd already threatened to rape children, and had now killed a woman who was in the wrong place at the wrong time, *being fucked in the ass by the wrong person.*

He could start questioning whether he was any better than them, but knew he was. He had a reason for doing all this. He was exacting vengeance. He hadn't started this, but he was damn sure going to fucking finish it. Unlike those bastards, he hadn't raped and murdered a kid. Threatening it was one thing; doing it was something else entirely. And Alice hadn't harmed anyone in her life. Barrett doubted the skinny bitch being fucked by Jessy could claim the same.

He didn't need to justify his actions, anyway. Vengeance wasn't about making clear, logical well thought-out decisions; it was about fucking payback! The three piles of human goo he'd left in his tracks so far qualified as exactly that, even if one of them hadn't been involved in the night in question.

While being homeless may have made Barrett invisible, being covered in blood and shit wouldn't. Despite the state of the grotty bathroom Barrett knew it was time for a long overdue shower. *Killing three people leaves quite the stink.*

He wasn't normally aroused by the vengeance he took, but decimating the nude couple to such a horrific degree had left him rock hard. Whacking off in their shower while they lay as a mix and match pile of human play-dough in the bedroom seemed like one last fun fuck you, in Barrett's increasingly unhinged mind.

By the time the cum drizzled down the eroded drain at the foot of the shower, he felt clean again, and ready to take his final vengeance.

He slipped on some fresh clothes he found which belonged to Jessy; they were a little wide, but mostly fit. Then he took a jacket which had been slung over the banister and concealed his crowbar inside. That, too, had been washed and dried, having been places no crowbar should ever have gone. A hint of the smell would always remain ingrained in the steel, but there wasn't anything he could do about that.

Barrett wasn't sure when the music had stopped and the sun had risen. He'd been too engaged in the destruction of Jessy and Mia to be aware of anything else going on around him. Someone could have walked in on him and he wouldn't have known, although their terrified screams would probably have alerted him.

He was fucking starving too. He hadn't eaten since before watching Eric at the greasy spoon the day before, which felt like a lifetime ago now.

A lot's happened since then.

He left the house unnoticed and walked a few streets over to grab some breakfast in a coffee shop. He couldn't remember the last time he'd been in one. It used to be his daily ritual, but not much from his previous life remained.

While drinking his caramel latte, he watched the world begin to wake. Little did they know three barbaric murders had taken place in close proximity during their slumber. Eric's body would surely be found soon, or may have already, but no one was going to be reporting the smell coming from Mia's place in a hurry; it was probably the norm.

Drinking this celebratory coffee at the half way point could have been mistaken for sheer fucking hubris, but Barrett was in too good a mood not to. He'd just destroyed two of the fuckers who raped and murdered his family, and now knew the location of the last two. A job well done, considering the last time the sun rose he'd been none the closer to finding any of them. He deserved the flavoured coffee and bacon roll, and even had a slice of lemon cake.

Then he set about finishing the job.

Vengeance Comes To Those Who Wait

Barrett felt a level of exhilaration coursing through his body which he'd never felt before. It was a mixture of nervous anticipation and delirium. He'd taken plenty of vengeance in the past, and had caused more carnage in the last twenty-four hours than he had the previous sixteen years, but something about this upcoming moment was extra special. More intoxicating.

While he fully blamed Eric and Jessy for their part in the vicious assault, and duly took his merciless retribution, these last two fuckers were the ones who'd stuck their putrid cocks in his wife and daughter. The ones who'd truly taken their lives. The other two were accomplices, and they paid dearly for their role, but these two were the ringleaders, who deserved their place burning in hell in tiny little pieces.

As they soon would be.

The gym was one of those old-school macho gyms you'd expect a young and hungry *Rocky Balboa* to be training at. It was stuck on a street corner with a dusty sign above the door: *T-Rex Urban Gym*. The logo was a dinosaur lifting dumbbells, and looking fucking badass doing it.

The whole vibe of the place was some red-blooded cliche where you'd have to know someone who already trained there in order to be let in, *or you'd get the fucking shit kicked out of you just for opening the door.* 'Outsiders not welcome,' may as well been sprayed on the side of the aging building.

By the time Barrett arrived in town, the gym was already open. He had no idea if Tex and Rick were inside, but it was clear from the clientele who were turning up he couldn't just waltz in there during opening hours and destroy the motherfuckers.

Every single one of the members looked like a fucking bear. The stink of sweat in the place probably rivalled the funk of Jessy's girl's place. A couple more muscle-bound guys arrived on their motorbikes and parked outside the front of the gym as Barrett watched the place began to fill. The gym was a joint to pump some serious iron, but Barrett had brought steel.

He squeezed the crowbar in his jacket, itching to use it but knew he couldn't just storm in there and unleash hell. He had to wait.

Patience is a virtue.

Instead, he took a sneaky peek inside as he walked by. He couldn't see much from the doorway, but it was clear there was a boxing ring and a bunch of equipment to the side. The dinosaur was appropriate; no modern gym looked anything like this anymore.

They probably jab slabs of meat in their grey hoodies in the back.

The place was a health and safety hazard from top to bottom, but no inspectors were about to walk in and close them down.

Barrett talked himself out of doubling back for another stroll-by and instead went to the cafe the other side of the road. *The Morning Brew.* It was another establishment stuck in time, the choice of coffee consisting of black or white. Barrett eventually ordered himself a black coffee from the crabby cafe owner and sat in the uncomfortable plastic chair by the window.

It had an unimpeded view of the gym doorway, so he began to stake the place out. Maybe not the most original plan, but it had always worked for him in the past.

The Morning Brew was packed full of construction workers all munching on their full English breakfasts. A sea of dirty safety vests sat between Barrett and the cafe owner, yet the old man still kept an eye on him. Outsiders were not a common sight around here, and anyone new was treated suspiciously.

The town had nothing to hide; it was just stuck in its ways and paranoid of the world changing around it.

Barrett could feel the old timer's stare burning into the back of his neck but tried to remain inconspicuous. He wasn't doing anything wrong, just sitting by the window drinking his piping hot black coffee. Asking for a caramel latte hadn't helped him blend in with the locals, but after giving in and having one earlier in the morning, he'd fancied another. It was the small pleasures in life.

Flavoured coffee and decimating people with a fucking crowbar.

He'd have to settle for bitter coffee and a long wait for the time being.

He rolled his tongue around the ulcers once again forming inside his cheeks and clicked his broken nose -- a habit he'd recently picked up. His arms ached from all the hell he'd unleashed overnight, but he hoped the coffee and adrenaline would perk him up. He knew his body was feeling rundown; overworked after such a long break between vengeances, but revenge was still to be taken, and he was at his final destination.

The street outside was the sort which hadn't changed in a hundred years. The houses looked old and crumbling, while the road was filled with potholes. Litter danced down the sidewalk and every shop was run by Ma and Pa. No chains had claimed this area yet; a rarity. Barrett figured it would only be a matter of time before the place got modernised like everywhere else, but for the moment he sat almost admiring the street time forget. This was exactly why the old man behind the counter was wary; they knew change would eventually arrive, and it wasn't welcome.

He wondered whether Tex and Rick had faced the same hostility when they set up shop. Or was this where they grew up? Could an outsider just buy the gym across the street and already have a loyal customer base? Or did they have history here?

Barrett wished he could ask the cafe owner; he imagined the grumpy old fuck knew everything about the town. But asking questions didn't seem wise. Barrett decided the rapists had a history with the place, *probably grew up a few roads over.* It made killing them here even more fitting, and brought a wicked smile to his lips.

When Rick finally emerged from the gym, Barrett's stomach tightened. Flashbacks of him raping Alice jumped into his mind, making him spill his coffee. He hadn't been prepared for the strong reaction, as he'd always taken everything in stride, and worked himself towards those sort of emotions. In the past, the violence had always been committed against him. He'd had minor reactions to Eric and Jessy, but had largely kept his cool, *it's all relevant.*

But seeing Rick brought out something more primal in Barrett. Another depth to his craving for vengeance. His powerful need for retribution and unwavering revenge. This cunt raped his beautiful loving wife in front of him! Shot his load in her, then took part in her murder. He had to fucking die.

Barrett wanted to storm over there and smash his face in with the crowbar, exhume his fucking soul, but Rick had company, standing alongside two bikers, shooting the shit. The skull and rose tattoo wrapped around his wrist was on display in the cold harsh daylight.

One of Barrett's eyes may never have been the same after briefly popping out, but the vision in the other was still ultra-sharp. The tattoo was practically flashing, a macabre beacon drawing his attention. He'd spent half a year searching for the design, and there it was. If Barrett wasn't going to smash Rick's fucking head in right away, the other urge was to ask him where he got the tattoo done, to see if he'd ever been close.

Wouldn't have mattered with them out the city anyway.

He also felt like he knew it was Rick before spotting the tattoo. Something deep inside spoke to him the moment he set eyes on the beast. Maybe it was some nuance in the way he carried himself. Or, more than likely in Barrett's mind, it was the fact they were connected now. You can't forget the person who you watched rape your wife, even if you never saw their face. Their destinies had become entwined that day. Their paths were always meant to cross again, and they had.

Barrett continued to observe Rick from the safety of the cafe as the last of the construction workers piled out. He'd steadied himself since his initial reaction and once again held the coffee in his hand. It was getting cold at this point, but it was only really a prop; he'd order another soon and continue his stakeout. Seeing Rick so far from where he'd been looking felt fortuitous. He couldn't imagine another set of circumstances which would have led him to this gym.

Fuck life finding a way, death does too! The Devil had his back. These motherfuckers were meant to die horribly at Barrett's hands; he really was destined to have his vengeance. He'd found the needle in the haystack, and now he was going to snap the needle in fucking half. His blood began to boil.

Ten minutes into the conversation, another man emerged, with *Tex* printed in large black letters across his white top.

Barrett could almost laugh. *Yep, this is definitely meant to be.* He was a big fucker, bigger than Barrett remembered. Clearly he'd been hitting his own weights. His gruff voice carried in the wind and penetrated the Morning Brew window as he joined the laughter and cursing alongside the others. The voice was exactly as Barrett remembered. The same aggressive ex-con-like roughness to it, although more jovial around friends, rather than people he intended to ruin.

More flashbacks infected Barrett's mind, not of his wife, but his daughter as she laid naked on the floor with that monster taking her virginity. Barrett had studied the look on Jade's face in the moment and had thought about it every day since. It was crystal clear, and extremely loud. He remembered the screams, the cries, the blood, and the loss. This asshole took everything from Jade, including eventually her life.

The two men responsible for the worst day in Barrett's existence were the width of a road away, both laughing and joking across the street like they didn't have a care in the world and weren't about to be fucking exterminated.

Rick looked in Barrett's direction. Just a casual glance, nothing more. It may not have even been at Barrett, more trying to work out whether he fancied a coffee or not. Barrett didn't break his stare. He didn't look away. Although he wasn't looking like the bum he'd been when he attacked Eric and Jessy, he wasn't looking like the man whose life they'd destroyed either. He doubted they'd recognise him, and couldn't give a flying fuck if they did.

Destroyed in one sense of the word anyway; in another, it could be argued they'd given him back his life. Diverted him back to the path he was meant to be walking. Family life had been a nice diversion, a short-term vacation, but long-term, it was a lie. Barrett was sure of that more than ever, now as he watched the pair.

Taking vengeance was what he was designed to do. Why else would he have his high pain threshold, insane recovery ability, and ironclad mindset? He was exactly where he was meant to be.

Rick looked away, but he'd be seeing Barrett again soon enough.

*

Barrett refilled his coffee several times as he watched various boneheaded assholes come and go from the gym. That was the only time he took his eyes off the place, and even then he kept looking back. The owner hadn't questioned him being in the cafe all day, and was kept busy by different locals popping in for a chat.

Not a single woman entered the intimidating gym during Barrett's surveillance, and it wasn't a mystery why, given the little he knew about Tex and Rick. Maybe women could sense the rape on them? Maybe they leered at any women they saw? Maybe they had a reputation, one which they rightfully deserved.

The lack of female clientele could have been something simpler. No women's locker-room, or the fucking stench of the place perhaps? But Barrett concluded it was because these fuck-heads like to rape women and children, so the women stayed as far away from them as possible. It seemed the most poignant answer.

They wouldn't have to worry much longer; soon the creeps would be in the ground. Or, rather, scattered around the fucking toxic gym.

He hadn't seen any other trainers during his time watching the place. Maybe there were others and it was their day off, or maybe it was just Tex and Rick running the show. He hoped for the latter; it would make what he was about to do simpler. Of course, he could stake them out longer if that wasn't the case. Follow them home. Attack them in their sleep, or outside their front doors. He could see if they had families and torment them, or at bare minimum make them aware of what cunts their husbands or fathers were.

There were a lot of options, and he'd considered them all in the last two years. He'd played back countless scenarios in his head. Some he'd been cold and calculated, others he'd been foolhardy and reckless. In every case he'd gotten his vengeance;

never once had he failed to take his pound of flesh.

The gym only got busier as the day progressed. They must have been teaching some kind of class, or having a fucking BBQ out back in the cold, as the place was bustling. More rough-looking tattooed dickheads kept arriving to get their sweat on. Every single one of them seemed chummy with Tex and Rick whenever they made an appearance out front; the pair really had endeared themselves with the local neanderthals since setting up shop here.

There has to be history.

Barrett started making up stories about each scumbag who arrived at the gym. They were all bad news. Wife-beaters. Abusers. Burglars. Gang members. They all did drugs, drank too much, and beat on *their* woman. They all raped and murdered, just like their besties Rick and Tex. *Pieces of shit, every last fucking one of them.* He imagined them all inside, causally chatting about who they'd beaten up and fucked. How they'd broken their missus' nose for not doing the washing up, or the cunt had dared question them smelling of a cheap hooker's perfume so they had to nut the slag.

He didn't for a second consider the possibility any of them could be decent men; how could they be with the company they kept?

As Barrett made up his stories, and stared daggers through the window anytime Tex or Rick made an appearance, he forgot about the old man behind the counter watching him like a hawk.

He'd been suspicious of Barrett the moment he'd walked in, and the distrust hadn't faded as the day drew to a close. It only magnified with each growl Barrett unknowingly emitted. He was coming across as a fucking psycho. The old man knew he was up to no good, even if he couldn't place what the deed was.

When no one other than Barrett was in the cafe, the Morning Brew owner disappeared out back and dialled the gym across the road.

Ten minutes later, there was a mass exit at the gym. Whatever was going on seemed to be over, as everyone began to make their way home.

Barrett watched as Tex and Rick chatted to several of the bikers at the door once more. Rick again glanced towards the cafe before returning to his conversation. Two of the bikers said their goodbyes before heading over to the cafe. Barrett ignored the meatheads as they entered and made a beeline for the counter.

He only had eyes for Rick and Tex. For vengeance.

He heard the pair in the background ordering a couple of coffees to go, but failed to register how close the sound of their voices were to him.

By the time he realised something was up, he got a cattle prod to the gut and fell to the floor as the electricity buzzed though his body.

"Tex wants a word with you," one of the bikers told Barrett as they dragged him by his arms out of the cafe.

Zap first, ask questions later.

I Will Have My Vengeance

The busy street had become quiet, not a soul in sight as the biker duo dragged Barrett across the road to the gym.

Barrett's body had stopped convulsing, but he didn't put up much of a struggle as he eyed his destination. Tex and Rick waited by the heavy door to usher the men inside, then locked up for the day.

The CLOSED sign occasionally swung around early for a good night out, or family events, but this was the first time they'd closed early for a more nefarious cause since opening the place. Tex and Rick really had intended to go on the straight and narrow, aside from the odd strong-arming to get what they needed when starting up, but now they were going to have to go off the books as their past caught up with them.

Rick never forgot a face. He had spotted the aggrieved husband and father in the cafe across the street earlier in the day. His suspicions were confirmed when the grouchy owner of the Morning Brew phoned him and told of some asshole mad-dogging them from the window.

He'd sent Chip and Dean across the street to fetch the cunt while they'd cleared the others out of the gym. Every one of their members would gladly have given the asshole a kicking, but that wasn't how Tex and Rick did business. This was their mess, and they would clean it up, like they should have two years ago.

Chip forcefully patted Barrett down before tossing him to the gym floor like he was nothing. He'd taken the crowbar from his jacket and carelessly discarded it behind him, seemingly unimpressed with the rusty weapon.

If only you knew what it had already done.

Chip ripped Barrett's shirt from his body - without Barrett

offering any resistance - and left the stranger laying bare-chested and embarrassed on the dusty gym floor.

"No wire," Chip announced to the others.

With Barrett disarmed and clean of any wire, Tex and Rick stood over him while Chip and Dean flanked to either side, in case Barrett tried to make a run for it; he wasn't going anywhere.

Despite his long history of vengeance, Barrett had never been in a real mano-a-mano fight before. He'd got his ass kicked, and he'd kicked plenty of ass in return, but not once had there ever been any to-and-fro. He was either jumped and had the fuck beaten out of him without ever trying to fight back, or he took swift one-sided deadly vengeance.

With the four large guys all standing around him, and no weapon to hand he knew he was in a real fight for the first time. It wasn't his plan, but he was relishing the opportunity.

After years of waiting, he was so close to the two men who raped and murdered his wife and daughter he could smell the sweat on them. He could see the yellows of their teeth; the hatred and constant anger in their eyes.

Men like them can never truly hide who they are.

He could see the skull rose tattoo up close and personal for the first time since the hand it was inked onto beat his wife.

After a two year search, he'd found them. They'd found him at the same time, but while he knew what they were capable of, they had absolutely no fucking idea what Barrett could do.

"After all this time, you still enjoy watching us?" Rick joked with a knowing smirk.

Thinks he's so fucking clever. He had his massive arms crossed, flexing his biceps as he stood over Barrett. The intimidation factor was high, but Barrett wasn't easily frightened. *The bigger they are the harder they fall.*

"Fuck you doing here?" Tex asked in his gruff aggressive

voice. While Rick was clearly amused by Barrett's odd re-emergence, Tex was in no mood to fuck around. They'd left this shit behind them when they set up the gym. Barrett was not a welcome reunion.

Chip gave Barrett a couple of kicks to the side, clearly trying to impress the two gym owners. "The man asked you a question," he grunted, as Barrett suppressed his grin at the feeling of being beaten once again.

It had been few and far between the last sixteen years, and the feeling was still intoxicating, but that wasn't what he was here for.

Rick shook his head, unimpressed with the feeble pile of shit at his feet. He let out a small laugh to go with the shake, *disappointing.* "Still a chicken shit, huh? I get it." He leant down to Barrett, hunched eye to eye, stroking his chin like some kind of thoughtful scholar as he continued to shake his head. "You accidentally caught sight of us and it all came flooding back? Got yourself all worked up? Balled your fists and stomped your feet like a little girl?" Rick mocked, clenching his own fists with a fake determined look on his face. "To do what, exactly…?"

Rick grinned like he had it all worked out, despite leaving the last bit hanging. He couldn't have found Barrett any less threatening if he tried. Barrett played his part by shrinking back further on the floor, his shoulders slumping in faux defeat. The little fight he'd shown left his body. He even started to shake. *Give me the Oscar straight fucking now.*

"You phone the pigs?" Tex barked, in his more direct style. He hadn't calmed over the last two years; if anything he sounded even more angry despite the years treating him well -- and him being the one in the wrong in the first place.

"I didn't phone the police," Barrett mumbled, like he regretted the decision - *which he didn't.*

"Tell anyone you're here?" Tex interrogated.

Barrett shook his head.

Rick couldn't quite believe the stupidity. "Too embarrassed? Scared? Dumb?"

Barrett didn't answer, just lowered his head further. It looked like he was practically begging at this point as he continued to play along. He made sure they all felt nice and comfortable around him. He could see it written across all their faces as they literally and figuratively looked down on him.

'Fucking pussy' they collectively thought. *Good.*

"So what's the deal? Your daughter want another ride?" Tex howled, showing the first sign of humour now he'd determined how absolutely fucking woeful Barrett was.

"She's dead. Killed herself." Tears flooded Barrett's eyes at the deadpan confession. He didn't need to fake them; they were one-hundred-percent real. The hurt was still inside him, even if it did sit next to unbridled excitement at the prospect of getting to rip these motherfuckers apart.

"Shame," was all Tex said. He left it open to interpretation whether he meant he was sorry she died so young, or shame he couldn't have another go at fucking the youngster. Barrett assumed it was the latter.

"She slit her wrists after what you assholes did to her," Barrett said, showing the first real sign of any aggression in his voice. He did, however, keep his eyes glued to the floor, not looking up at the men who wrecked his life.

He'd never had to put on a performance before and found himself enjoying it. They really thought he was meek and pathetic, and most importantly, helpless. He could visibly see all four of them letting their guard down. He hadn't expected to be in this position, as it was never part of his plan to get ambushed by them. Fuck, he'd even killed Mia to avoid this exact sort of situation. But now he was in such a vulnerable position, he could use it. He could make it all part of his ultimate vengeance.

Clearly, Chip and Dean didn't know the full story, but they weren't about to question Tex and Rick. Whatever happened had happened; they weren't going to get involved. They would protect their friends, however, no matter the crime. Barrett knew the odds weren't in his favour. Then again, they never were.

He began to slowly climb to his feet and they allowed it. After all, what the fuck was a so-called man who allowed his wife and daughter to be raped and murder without lifting a finger going to do?

Barrett studied Chip and Dean, then smiled as he locked eyes with Tex. "I see you've replaced Eric and Jessy already. That's quick work."

"What'd you say?" Tex eyed Barrett, as if trying to work out the odd fucking statement. Having any time to think about it, he'd assume Barrett would believe these two were the other two guys involved

Barrett's lips curled into a daring 'you heard me' gesture, giving his game away a little, but still leaving enough mystery as to what exactly he was capable of, and what he'd already done. He was enjoying himself.

Rick's jovial demeanour faded, suddenly becoming wary of the pathetic former husband and father, wondering what he was hiding.

Without warning, Tex unleashed a vicious haymaker, dropping Barrett to the deck with the meaty right fist. He then grabbed Barrett by the ears and lifted him, before tossing him into the boxing ring with ease. Chip and Dean cheered him on.

Rolling into the ring, Tex gave Barrett a few kicks before straddling him and punching him square in the face several more times, crunching his features. No trash talk, no wasted shots. He was all fucking business as he busted Barrett's jaw and blackened his eyes. Leaving Barrett a bloody, spluttering mess lying in the middle of the ring, he pulled his mobile out and phoned Eric.

No answer.

He phoned Jessy. Still no answer.

Tex shook his head to Rick with each unanswered call. He tried Eric's wife next and was greeted by hysterics. Tucking the phone away he relayed the frantic conversation to Rick.

"Eric never came home last night, and early this morning they found a body near his place."

They looked at each other, confused, and slightly worried. Both suddenly wondering if there was more than met the eye to the loser lying in the middle of their ring.

Tex's attention turned back to Barrett.

"What did you do?"

Barrett just smiled…

… then reached up and grabbed Tex's sweaty balls through his gym shorts and squeezed. Hard!

Tex shrieked as Barrett kept on squeezing until one of the fuckers popped in his hand like a pus-filled pimple.

The other three piled into the ring, but Barrett was already rolling out. Chip was the first to catch up with him and they exchanged blows outside the ring.

Chip had fucking hammers for hands, with each blow leaving a dent, but Barrett could take it. Barrett punched back and knocked Chip away. Chip definitely felt the pain more than Barrett, despite being able to hit the harder.

By the time Chip realised Barrett had made his way to the discarded crowbar, it was too late. Thinking he'd caught Barrett good, he sent him tumbling to the floor, but Barrett sprung back to his feet with the weapon in hand. He wasted no time stabbing the pointy end into Chip's shoulder, before hooking the claw side in his mouth and ripping his cheek wide open, sending blood spraying across the gym mats.

"Holy fuck!" was all Dean could shout as he reached the mess. Half of Chip's face looked like a grisly cut of uncooked meat. He searched for a weapon as Barrett made a beeline for him next.

The only thing nearby was a dumbbell, so he grabbed it and began swinging it like a club. Barrett avoided all but one swing, the last one catching him on the elbow, but by then he was close enough to Dean to cause his own damage.

He brought the claw end of the crowbar down across Dean's face, planting it into his eye socket. He tore away the orbital bone as he yanked to free the weapon. Without the bone structure underneath, the eye slipped from its position and dangled, allowing Dean a view of his shoes with one eye while looking straight ahead with the other.

He didn't have to time to freak out, as a follow up with the crowbar knocked him cold and left a sizeable indent on his skull.

"You crazy fuck!" Rick screamed, launching himself from the ring

The crowbar was knocked from Barrett's hand as Rick landed on him, raining down punches, cracking Barrett's face further with blow after blow, doubling the damage Tex had already caused. Nose re-broken for the umpteenth time, already busted jaw dislocated, other eye blackened. Rick went feral on the asshole who'd just butchered his friends.

While Barrett was enjoying the pain of the beating, it wasn't what he was here for, and he couldn't risk losing the fight.

Going against his natural instincts, Barrett put his arms up in defence hoping to deflects some of the spicy blows for the first time in his life. The room was spinning and his face felt both fractured and on fire. *Rick can fucking punch!*

Barrett grabbed the fallen crowbar and swung the claw end

into Rick's thigh, tearing into the muscle and momentarily stopping the onslaught. Rick's hand instinctively went to the pain, giving Barrett a chance to punch him in the fucking face.

Barrett climbed back to his feet, accidentally stepping on Dean's eyeball -- it had finally come loose from the broken socket and ended up on the floor, squelching under Barrett's foot. Wiping the blood from his ruined face, he seized the fallen dumbbell Dean had attempted to hit him with, slid back into the ring, and swung the heavy dumbbell at Tex's head before Tex could get his arms up to divert the blow.

The sickening thud of dumbbell on skull echoed throughout the gym as the weight changed the shape of Tex's head. No sooner had he gotten to his feet than he was back down on the canvas, this time for the count. Barrett stamped on his ribs several times, hearing the bones crack beneath his feet. He punted Tex's mouth, busting it opening and sending teeth flying. Another stomp to the face cracked Tex's nose, while the follow up dislodged a couple more broken teeth.

Having made quick work of his daughter's rapist, Barrett left him lying half-dead in the ring, promising himself he'd finish the bent-cock fucker last.

Despite the sudden, vicious assault, such a level of restraint was one Barrett didn't normally show. Once he started, he normally couldn't stop, but this cunt needed more than one beating before death. Tex had raped his daughter and killed his wife. Reshaping his fucking head, breaking a few ribs, and dislodging a couple of teeth was not nearly enough vengeance. Not by a fucking long shot.

Barrett set his sights back on Rick, who was unsuccessfully trying to pry the crowbar from his ruined thigh having regained some of his bearing after the ferocious punch. His hands were shaking as blood carried on pouring from the hideous gash. Barrett helped free the devastating weapon with a reckless tug, which brought a chunk of thigh meat with it.

With the crowbar free, Barrett then proceeded to do what he did best and went fucking berserk on Rick before the rapist had the chance to beg him to stop. It wouldn't have mattered; he wasn't fucking stopping. Barrett viciously brought the crowbar up and down in a crazed outburst, leaving no part of Rick untouched as he attempted to break every single fucking bone in his cruel body.

Barrett flipped Rick over and worked his way up the rapist's back, jackhammering the crowbar into each vertebrae, seeing if he could break them. He wasn't about to check the results, though; *the fun was in the trying.*

He ripped Rick's shorts from his body and rolled him back over, then smashed the crowbar into his dick. There was no attempt to claw his manhood off like he had Jessy; just cause maximum hurt while the rape tool was attached.

His blows with the crowbar became aimless as the insanity continued; he was just trying to cause pain wherever they landed. One moment, Rick's shins were being splintered; the next, a testicle ruptured. Then an elbow was dislocated. Before Rick lost feeling in his legs, Barrett clawed at his toes one at a time, scraping the skin off them like meat from ribs. He followed it up by repeating the process with Rick's fingers, except it wasn't just the skin which came off; he severed half of them.

Blood, piss, shit and vomit exploded from the various ruined parts of Rick's body as his agonising and pleading screams brought no leniency. Death was the only saviour he could hope for now, but it wasn't coming just yet. Barrett discarded the crowbar and started raining punches down on Rick crushing his face underneath the wild blows as memories of his wife being raped continued to fuel the unsparing assault.

Rick's nose caved in. His eyes swelled shut. His mouth was busted wide open with plenty of teeth dribbling out. His ears stung, which was about the least of all his worries. Barrett could see his wife's tormentor's face starting to shift and distort under his fists as more and more of it was broken.

His own face was pretty fucked up to, and his hands were starting to show bone by now, but he looked in model condition compared to the mangled heap of shit beneath him. He wasn't done yet. Barrett stood and stamped down hard on Rick's wrist. He left his foot holding it in place as he retook the crowbar and brought the clawed end down, cutting through the veins and burying itself into the bone. A little more pressure, and he could probably sever the hand, but that wasn't his agenda.

He dug the claw bar under the skin, ripping away at it from beneath while blood squirted from the exposed veins. It wouldn't be long before Rick bled out, but Barrett didn't need long to peel off the top layer of skin from the wrist, separating it from the rest of the hand, liberating the skull and rose tattoo.

He was still tempted to ask Rick where he got it done, but there wasn't time. Instead, he grabbed Rick's busted mouth and pulled it open, allowing several more loose teeth to spill out. He stuffed the tattooed skin inside before closing Rick's mouth again. Let him could choke on the fucking thing; it seemed fitting.

Barrett held his mouth shut while Rick instinctively struggled to breathe. Barrett knew the struggle was involuntary, because no fucking way was he coherent.

Blood cascaded from the skinned wrist. He was probably at least partially paralysed, judging by his weakness and the damage Barrett had inflicted on his spine. At least three quarters of the bones in his body were broken and he looked uglier than month old pizza. Even if he could survive, there was zero point to it ... not that he'd have to worry about it. He had seconds left at best.

Rick's fruitless fight barely lasted to the end of Barrett's thoughts. His body stopped flopping around and accepted defeat. The rise and drop of his chest came to a stand still. His eyes rolled back and his heart stopped beating. Barrett wasn't sure what precise element had killed him; whether he'd choked to death, or bled out.

Doesn't matter. The end result is the same.

He rammed the crowbar into Rick's stomach and cracked open what was left of his rib cage so he could get to the heart. It took him a minute, but he reached it.

He yanked the useless organ from Rick's body and threw it at his face, before stomping on them both together, trying to explode them like a watermelon. Much like Dean's eyeball, the heart made a very satisfying squelch, even if it didn't quite explode.

Man that felt good. He hoped Alice's parents would be proud of the finish, after what the scumbag had done to their pride and joy.

Barrett took a long look at his handiwork. Rick wasn't recognisable as the man who'd been laughing and joking with his gym buddies all day. You could ask each and every one of them who the mess on the floor was and they wouldn't know.

Ironically, the only thing Barrett had used to even identify him to begin with was probably the cause of his death, the peeled off patch of tattooed skin stuffed down his throat.

Poetic.

Dean had stopped breathing at some point during Rick's dissection, and Barrett put an end to Chip's life with a golf swing of the crowbar to the back of his head. Fuck them both.

Now for the last one.

Barrett turned to the ring ...

... but Tex was gone.

He heard a door swing open at the other end of the gym and smiled at Tex's futile escape attempt. Barrett decided he was going to take his time with Tex. He'd promised himself that every other time too, and it had never panned out as planned. But this time he'd try and show some restraint.

He's the last of them, after all.

He marched towards the door -- it led to a back office -- but couldn't see Tex through the big window as he approached. *Probably hasn't made it up off the floor.* Surprising that Tex had the wherewithal to even crawl to the office, given the disturbing shape of his fucking head, and the rest of the destruction caused. He'd shown some heart, but Barrett would soon rip it out. *Just like Rick's*

Barrett smugly walked through the office door, feeling like a million bucks and high on vengeance ...

... until the world exploded with a loud BANG as Tex blasted him in the head at point-blank range with a sawed-off shotgun.

Barrett always saw himself as invincible, but it turned out he wasn't.

Worst of all, he hadn't completed his vengeance.

An Eternity of Vengeance

Barrett felt the ground burning beneath him, like he was lying on hot coals.

The air was bone dry, similar to what you'd find in a desert, but deserts were rarely ablaze.

He was surrounded by columns of fire fifty feet high, behind which ranged an endless vista of volcanoes, spewing out bubbling pits of lava teeming with thousands upon thousands of forlorn faces and outstretched pleading arms. They all swirled in unbearable anguish, burnt to a crisp as they were constantly swallowed and regurgitated by the impossibly red fire encompassing them.

The screeches from the pits were deafening, but no one was listening; no one was coming to help them out of the inferno.

Barrett climbed to his feet and took in the surreal surroundings.

It wasn't the fucking gym anymore, that was for sure. Horned demons and fiery winged creatures whipped and guided those lucky enough not to be burning in the pits to various stony paths at the bottom of the infinite volcanoes. The whips they used were spiked and sharp; every lash drew blood at best, or at worst took a fucking limb from the captives as they were led towards eternal punishments. The detached limbs were gathered up by smaller demons, for what use wasn't immediately clear, but something deep inside Barrett's mind told him they'd end up in a stew

An orchestra of moans and wails reverberated from every angle, not just from the burning pits or marching damned souls. Agony was the soundtrack of this forsaken place. Every one of the figures being guided towards the volcanoes was naked and emaciated. Skin and bone.

Barrett looked down at his own body. He wasn't naked like them; instead, was wrapped in a tattered cloak - although had lost his boots at some point. He wondered how he could look down, what with his very last feeling being one of having his fucking head explode. He reached up to touch whatever rested on his shoulders, and felt the undeniable texture of bone. A rotting bare skull devoid of skin had replaced his blown-off face.

Ahead of him was a path with a tall jagged rocky archway overhead. With no other option, he began to walk the scorching path. His bare feet hissed with every step. His arms sizzled. His replacement skull felt heavy and hazy.

Still, he was alone, walking on his own. He wasn't stuck in the fiery pits, nor was he being guided naked and abused to an evil looking volcano for fuck knows what nefarious purpose.

For the moment, at least, he was still Barrett. But there was no question about it ... he was in Hell.

The path felt endless, but it gave Barrett time to think. He hadn't had a moment to reflect on his recent vengeance like he normally would, but part of that was because he hadn't finished the job.

He was only three quarters through. Barrett had fucked Tex up for sure, but he hadn't delivered the killer blow. Tex would never be the same again, but he was still alive, unlike Alice and Jade… and now Barrett himself.

He'd messed up. He'd walked right into the room like he was invincible, and part of the reason for it was he believed he was. *How fucking arrogant.*

He'd let his family down. Without finishing his quest for vengeance, Alice and Jade's deaths were meaningless. He may as well have saved them, if he couldn't bask in the euphoria of avenging them.

Three out of four isn't bad, but it's not enough.

He wanted to feel the tears streaming down his face as he tormented himself with his monumental failure, but skulls don't cry. That only made him more angry, more disappointed in his shortfall.

Barrett always got his vengeance; this wasn't acceptable.

The images of Alice and Jade being raped were magnified in the heat of Hell. The beads of sweat and tears on them were crystallised as the assault replayed on loop in his head. It wasn't even his doing; Hell was projecting the reruns for him. The sounds they made haunted his new skull. Every scream was dialled up. Both cried his name at the top of their lungs. They begged for him to help, and he promised he would… but he hadn't then, and he hadn't now.

He'd allowed Alice's killer and Jade's rapist to live. To fucking *live*! How could he betray his loving family like this? How could he let Alice die knowing he couldn't even exact revenge? His baby girl died in the bathtub knowing her dad was a failure, and she'd been right.

Vengeance means nothing if you don't take it.

Barrett collapsed to the red-hot ground. For the first time ever, the pain was unbearable. The memories too vivid. They were rusty spikes through his mind. He felt like he was there all over again and everything was cranked up to the max.

He could see every detail of Tex's crooked vile cock as it slammed into his beautiful young daughter. Every pubic hair, every blotch on the skin. He could smell the spunk building, see the pre-cum reflecting his daughter's brutalised cunt. It was in 3D. 4K. Complete with smell-o-vision, and cinematic quality surround-sound. He really was there all over again. It couldn't have felt more real. It was more overwhelming now than when the fucking rape actually happened.

Jade's eyes were abnormally wide and full of so much pain. She had already entered her own hell as each thrust drove deeper inside her young body.

No wonder she killed herself.

Barrett couldn't bear it, and he wasn't the one who had endured it. He could see the life exiting her eyes as that asshole pumped his twisted dick into her. Barrett felt *her* pain, not *his*. He could always handle physical pain, and emotional pain had been a welcome anguish over the last two years.

But the pain his fourteen-year-old daughter felt while she was being raped was too much for Barrett to comprehend. *And he'd allowed it!* It was harrowing. Hell had made her torture a permanent part of him. Going forward, he'd forever feel her suffering. He'd feel the agony his beautiful sweet innocent daughter suffered, agony which even he considered too much.

How could I have let it happen? Still, the tears wouldn't come from the unfamiliar decaying skull which was now Barrett's head.

Barrett wasn't sure how much time passed, but somehow he made it back to his feet and carried on along the path of torment.

The vile visions of Jade were replaced by visions of Alice. He felt her heartbreak and hurt too. Then, Barrett felt the torture he'd put others through. The beatings he'd given the wannabe rapists. The fire which took the lives of innocents, as well as those he'd judged guilty. Every sin he'd committed in the name of vengeance attacked him as he continued his long endless trek.

If Barrett thought he craved pain and suffering, he was getting the purest version possible, as Hell unleashed undiluted misery on him.

His legs continued to carry him forward as his mind began to crumble. His best thoughts had always been of vengeance, they were his most treasured moments. Now, those thoughts were being used against him. The ecstasy of retribution was being corrupted. All the 'good' he'd done was being used to destroy his fragile mind.

Barrett needed to fight it. He needed to do what he'd always done, and embrace the pain. Own it. *Could this be an even higher level of enduring suffering to use?* At the moment it was crippling, but if he could weaponise it?

He stopped moving without thinking why. He realised his 'eyes' had been closed, and opened whatever resembled them now.

In front of him was a towering throne of meat and bone. Twisted. terrified faces and body parts were wielded together to form the seat. It only made sense that, sitting upon the satanic throne, was the Devil himself.

Part of Barrett knew this was what awaited at the end of the path. He didn't know how long he'd been walking; time had lost all meaning. But he knew deep down this was always going to be what waited.

The Devil towered, immense. Huge horns stuck from his head, and he had that evil face which was always depicted. Large red wings protruded from his enormous back and a huge girthy phallus swung proudly between his legs.

It had to be said, the Devil looked exactly like the Devil. *Had people come back in order for the accounts to be this accurate?*

He held a trident made of thick bone, and Barrett had to admit, it looked pretty fucking cool, and damn right evil. The Devil's appearance didn't disappoint; he was the real deal.

"I didn't finish my vengeancc."

They hadn't been Barrett's planned words. In fact, he was surprised he could even talk, realising he hadn't tried during his long journey. But those were the words which instantly escaped whatever now qualified as his mouth.

"Not my fault," the Devil responded, with a booming voice that commanded instant respect. It was the kind of voice which would make most men quiver, but Barrett had never seen himself as most men. "I've already given you a second chance, and you used it to play house."

"That was real?" Barrett asked, thinking back to the feverish dreams he'd had while comatose. They'd felt real at the time, but surely they couldn't have been?

"As real as you standing here right now."

"Then you can send me back again," Barrett demanded. It wasn't a polite request.

The Devil shook his head as he looked down at the puny, irate man beneath him. He'd taken a liking to Barrett, and the cruelty he'd demonstrated above, but he had no patience for disrespect.

Barrett could sense he'd overstepped his mark. "I need to complete my vengeance. It can't end like this..." he trailed off.

It was his fault it had ended like this, but given a chance, he could fix it. He could make sure Alice's and Jade's deaths meant something by killing Tex in the most barbaric way possible.

"You want to make a deal with the Devil?" the supreme evil mused with a knowing grin and a raised eyebrow. He may have been the ruler of Hell and known as evil personified, but even he couldn't resist a good pun.

Barrett nodded. *What've I got to lose?*

The Devil considered the proposal. He didn't need to be cutting deals - being the overlord of Hell and all - but a soul given was so much juicier than a soul taken, and it wasn't every day someone handed their soul to him personally.

He was the fucking Devil after all! Plus, he did like Barrett, and the thought of breaking such a stubborn man made the Devil's spine tingle. *He'll know true pain.*

"I'll grant you your vengeance, but in return, you will belong to me."

"Deal," Barrett answered without hesitation. He didn't need

a second to think about it, or the consequences; that was a problem for the future.

What he needed right now was vengeance. Tex had to die the cruelest way possible, at his hands.

The Devil produced a contract from thin air and laid it before Barrett to sign.

"It needs to be signed in blood," the Devil told him with a smirk.

Of course it does.

Barrett cut his hand on one of the bones sticking from the Devil's throne and signed the contract without reading it. It didn't matter what it said. As long as he could get his vengeance, nothing else mattered. He'd gladly sign his soul away to Satan if it meant he could finish the job. His addiction to vengeance had never felt stronger, now it was coming to its conclusion.

With the agreement signed, the Devil produced Tex from behind the throne just as quickly as he'd done with the contract.

Tex was a fucking mess. His deformed skull had turned black and his eyes were rolled back in his head. Dried black blood stuck to the bottom of his scrotum from his ruptured testicle. The ribs on display from his naked body were all kinds of blues and purples. His mouth was a gaping hole. All the injuries correlated with the beating Barrett had already carried out, just with time passed, and Hell's own exaggeration.

"I don't understand?" Barrett questioned.

The Devil grinned. It was a wicked grin only he was capable of displaying. He was not an entity to be trusted, yet somehow people still turned to him when their desperation reached its limits. When there was no other option left, and consequences be damned. They still sold their souls without ever truly understanding his unrivalled manipulation.

"He died right after you," the Devil said, with a sinister

laugh leaving his wicked mouth, knowing he'd just duped Barrett. "You had your vengeance after all."

Barrett smiled. *Thank fuck!* It hadn't been for nothing.

He'd never been afraid of death, but the idea of not completing his vengeance haunted him. Ruined him. Destroyed the very fabric of his being.

But he had taken it. Alice and Jade's killers were all dead. Every last one of those mother-fucking scumbag assholes were stuck in Hell with him right now.

The blissful high he'd been denied hit like unfiltered joy injected directly into his veins. *My fucking God it is incredible!* His whole body felt ablaze with euphoria, even his replacement head.

While stuck in Hell, Barrett was truly experiencing Heaven. He'd remember and relive this feeling until his end of days. Well, beyond that, all things considered...

A new thought struck Barrett. "Can I kill him again?"

The Devil shrugged and tossed Tex in Barrett's direction. After all, he liked the idea of seeing the man's work in person. A live performance, as it were.

"After you're done, you belong to me," he reaffirmed.

Barrett tore a bone from the throne - without even asking - and began the process of turning Tex into paste, one muscle at a time.

Slow, just like I promised myself.

He had no clue how long he was at it; time down there didn't work the same. It might have been days by the time Tex could fit in a bucket.

However, a bucket was too good for that raping, murdering, piece of shit. Once there was nothing left but a puddle of Tex, Barrett kicked the viscera into the fiery pit and watched the liquid sizzle before he handed himself over to the Devil.

Job done. Alice and Jade could rest in peace, and Barrett had his vengeance. It was all he ever wanted.

*

Every moment of Barrett's existence after getting his vengeance was spent in constant torment.

The Devil tore him apart and rebuilt him over and over. Boiled his fucking bones. Ripped Barrett's limbs off and shoved them back together in all the worse ways. Flayed his skin and burnt his exposed nerves in the lava.

He tore Barrett's cock off and made him eat it time and time again. Buggered him relentlessly with his enormous elephant cock, and passed him around the other demons as they all took their turn shredding his asshole and spitting their flaming jizz and piping hot liquid shit deep inside every hole Barrett possessed.

They made several new ones too, including an eye socket. Every part of his body was party to unbridled trauma. Unrelenting torture.

And, in time, Barrett learnt to love it.

He learnt to love the humiliation and violence. He endured each and every fuck, making note of the demons who came and went. He memorised every limb snapped, every muscle shredded, every cut made and bone broken.

He suffered greater than any man who'd ever walked the Earth, and all for the Devil's amusement. Eternal suffering, the Devil told him.

But what the Devil didn't know was, at the end of the eternal suffering, Barrett promised himself there would be retribution.

He always got his vengeance!

The End

Books by Stephen Cooper

Abby Vs The Splatploitation Brothers: Hillbilly
Farm
Near Death
Blood-Soaked Wrestling
The Rot
Not Four Children
Elephant Cock (Godless Exclusive Novelette)
Ensuring Your Place In Hell
Hack
Addicted To Vengeance

www.splatploitation.com

Printed in Great Britain
by Amazon

33958787R00075